Booford was asleep near the door of his house, but he hopped to his feet and barked crazily when we crossed the road. Edward stopped at the edge of the yard. "Booford?" he said. "An ugly name for an ugly dog."

Sometimes Edward is too honest. "He's not ugly," I said. I cupped Booford's face between my hands and kissed him on the forehead.

"Are you crazy?" Edward asked. "Can't you read? 'Beware of Dog.'" He stepped backward onto the road, frowning.

"That sign is a fake. This dog is nice.

"Don't listen to Edward," I whispered in Boo's ear. "You are a beautiful dog." Booford wagged his tail and jumped up and put his paws around my waist.

The Booford Summer

by Susan Mathias Smith
Illustrated by Andrew Glass

CLARION BOOKS

New York

Clarion Books
a Houghton Mifflin Company imprint
215 Park Avenue South, New York, NY 10003
Text copyright © 1994 by Susan Mathias Smith
Illustrations copyright © 1994 by Andrew Glass
The illustrations were executed in pencil and wash.
The text was set in 12-point Palatino.
Book design by Carol Goldenberg

www.houghtonmifflinbooks.com

Printed in the U.S.A.

Library of Congress Cataloging-in-Publication Data

Smith, Susan Mathias
    The Booford summer / by Susan Mathias Smith; pictures by Andrew
Glass.
        p.   cm.
    Summary: Ten-year-old Hayley worries about the dog across the street,
whose moody owner keeps him tied up and never walks him.
    ISBN 0-395-66590-6   PA ISBN 0-618-43245-0
    [1. Dogs—Fiction. 2. Animals—Treatment—Fiction.] I. Glass, Andrew, ill.
II. Title.
    PZ7.S65942Bo   1994
    [Fic]—dc20   93-27925

CIP
AC

MP 10 9 8 7 6 5 4

*Dedicated, with love and respect, to
my dad, Charles Edward Mathias
and
my friend, Richard West Kay, VMD*

Contents

The
Booford Summer

1. Booford

Booford was painted in white letters over the door of the doghouse. Some of the paint was cracked and peeling, but there was enough left of each letter for me to read the word.

"Booford," I said aloud. That's a funny name, I thought, and laughed. Booford must have heard my laugh because he barked and ran from inside his doghouse straight toward me. A short chain jerked him to a stop before he reached my feet.

He was still barking sharply. His teeth were big and kind of scary. Still, I like animals and I wanted to be his friend. So, I backed away a few steps, saying over and over in a soft voice, "Hello, Booford . . . Booford . . . Hello, Booford . . . Booford . . ."

Suddenly Booford's bark changed to a whimper, and he tilted his head to one side and stared at me. Very carefully, I stretched my hand toward him. Very slowly, he stretched his head toward my hand. Finally, his wet nose touched my fingertips and he sniffed.

"That's cat you smell," I said. "I have five cats. I don't have a dog."

Booford was not a very pretty dog. He was tall and bony and had odd-shaped white spots on a brown coat. He had long, floppy ears and a skinny, drooping tail. His face had deep lines. His eyes were big and brown and might have been pretty, but they were kind of sad.

Booford belonged to Mr. Wood, who had moved into the house across the back road. Just yesterday, my cat Hairy and I had sat on the front porch steps and watched movers unload the dog and doghouse and furniture and many boxes.

The front door of Mr. Wood's house opened. A big man came out the door and marched down the stairs and across the yard past me. I guessed he was Mr. Wood. He carried a hammer and a sign.

"Hi," I said. "I'm Hayley Larken and I live across the road. Right over there." I pointed to my family's house.

Mr. Wood didn't say a word. He didn't even smile.

"I'm Hayley," I repeated a little louder, thinking maybe Mr. Wood couldn't hear well.

Holding a nail between his teeth, Mr. Wood placed the sign on the tree to which Booford was tied. With a thick, hairy arm he raised the hammer and pounded the nail into the tree. BEWARE OF DOG, the sign said in big, black letters.

Mr. Wood finally spoke. "Can you read, kid?"

I nodded.

Mr. Wood turned and almost stomped back into the house.

"Bye, Booford," I mumbled, and I ran across the back road, through our yard, up the steps, and into the house.

Dad was in the kitchen drinking coffee. "A monster lives across the road," I announced. "He's big and hairy and hates children."

"He's chained or tied, isn't he?" Dad asked.

"Daddy," I said. "I mean Mr. Wood is a big, hairy monster."

"Hayley, it's six-thirty on a Monday morning. Lots of people are big, hairy monsters at six-thirty on a Monday morning." Dad put his thumbs in his ears, wiggled his fingers, and snapped his teeth at me.

"Oh, Dad," I said, trying not to laugh. "You don't make a very good monster. I'm not three years old, you know."

———

4

"Seriously," Dad said, "don't bother Mr. Wood. He probably has a lot of unpacking to do. You help your mom today. Pull weeds in the garden or something." He swallowed the last of his coffee and got up. "See you," he said. The back door banged shut behind him and immediately reopened. "And," he added, "try not to find any more stray cats."

"But I don't find them . . . they find me."

Dad winked at me. "I know," he whispered. "I know." The door banged shut again, and I heard Dad's car leave the driveway.

I fixed myself a glass of chocolate milk and two slices of toast with butter and grape jelly. I stirred the chocolate mix into the milk without hitting the spoon on the glass because I had just realized that, in spite of all the noise Dad and I had been making, my mom must still be asleep. She teaches English at the high school, and this was her first day of summer vacation. She had gone to school on Saturday to finish grading exams, and she had even gone back on Sunday after church to file papers and take down the bulletin board.

Today, knowing my mom, she would start what she called spring cleaning. Nobody else's mom spring-cleaned. Not one single fifth grade mom. But my mom began it every year on her first day of vacation. She washed every window in our house, organized every drawer in every dresser and every desk, and waxed all the floors. She cleaned the whole house, top to bottom, and everything in between.

I didn't mind doing chores, but I preferred being outside, planting green beans or even pulling weeds, to waxing and dusting and straightening. Maybe she would sleep late, I thought hopefully.

After I had eaten breakfast, I fed the cats, as I did first thing every morning and again at night. I opened three cans of food to divide among the five cats. Smokey eats in the kitchen; Dixie eats on the back porch; and Roby, Hairy, and Pinkie eat in the carport in the summer and on the back porch in the winter.

While the cats ate, I pulled Dad's big, green lawn chair out of the shade of the carport and into the morning sun in the front yard. I lay back and closed my eyes. It was probably only seven o'clock, but already the sun felt warm on my face and bare legs.

Suddenly, I heard Booford barking. I opened my eyes and watched Mr. Wood pour water into a large dish and some dry food into another. "Get back, dog!" Mr. Wood shouted. He sounded mean. Booford bounced up and down and lunged toward Mr. Wood, but Mr. Wood stuck out his arm and Booford backed away. Then Mr. Wood got into his truck, and bits of gravel flew as he left the driveway.

When his truck had disappeared over the hill on Route 11, I ran across the road. Booford met me at the end of his chain and jumped up and put his paws around my waist. "It's okay," I said aloud. "I'll be your friend. Now eat your breakfast."

I pulled away and raced back across the road. Mr. Wood could have gone to work, or he might only have gone to the store for coffee. I didn't think I should be in his yard when he got back.

I sat back down on the lawn chair and watched Booford, who was lying in the grass watching me. Poor Booford, I thought. What could I do?

Whiskers and a wet nose touched my cheek. "Hello, Smokey," I said.

Smokey was the first cat to live with my family. He is white with orange ears, and he has orange rings around his tail. His eyes are a light, crystal clear blue. Before I was born, Smokey lived with Mom and Dad. I'm ten. Smokey is eleven.

My parents got Smokey in Alaska while Dad was in the Air Force there. The people who lived in the downstairs apartment owned Smokey, and then they had a baby. Smokey kept trying to sleep with the baby, so they gave Smokey to my dad. When I was little, I pushed Smokey around in my doll carriage.

Smokey likes to be outside during the day, but he usually sleeps with me. Sometimes at night, I hear picky noises under my bed. I lean over the side of the bed, and there is Smokey hanging upside down by his claws from the covering on the box spring, peering at me.

Dixie became our second cat. She is small and white with big splotches of yellow and black. She came from the high school Dumpster. I was on the bus one morning, on the way from the high school where Mom teaches to the middle school, when I first saw her. At supper that evening, I told Mom and Dad about the kitty at the Dumpster. Mom had already seen her. She said that the cat would be fine eating leftovers from the school lunches. I said, "What happens when summer comes and there are no school lunches?" Mom said somebody would take her home before then. I said, "What somebody?" Dad said to watch her, "Just in case." "Just in case of what?" Mom had asked, but nobody answered her.

The very next evening, when I got off the bus at the high school, there sat Dixie huddled against the green Dumpster, her mouth bleeding. I grabbed her and ran to Mom's classroom where she was grading papers. She started to yell when she saw the cat in my arms, but then she saw the blood and we hurried to Dr. Rhodes's office.

Dixie lives on the clothes dryer on the porch. I think she is afraid of the other cats. Sometimes I make her go outside because I think she must be bored, but she doesn't want outside. She wants to sit on the clothes dryer.

Hairy became our third cat. Hairy was Edward's cat. Edward is my best friend. Edward's sister Margaret is allergic to cats. Margaret isn't that allergic, but their mother worries and fusses about every little thing. The cat had to go. I had to take him because I was Edward's friend and because I lived next door, which meant that Edward could visit every day.

Mom likes Hairy. He is fluffy and black and white and beautiful. He looks huggable, but he isn't. No one can hold him, and except for Pinkie, he doesn't even like the other cats. Whenever he is near them, his green eyes turn angry, and he wants to fight. Sometimes I call him Hairy Monster.

Pinkie became our fourth cat. Pinkie belonged to a lady in town who raises Siamese cats. When I rode my bike by her house, she opened the door and yelled at me to stop. Pinkie was standing in the doorway. She pushed him out the door with her foot. "Do you want this cat?" she said. "I don't like black cats." I picked Pinkie up and held him under my sweatshirt as I pushed my bike home. Mom said no. Dad said no. Since it was dark, Dad took Pinkie back to the lady's house. When he came back a half hour later, he still had Pinkie. Mom said no again. Dad said for Mom to take Pinkie back herself. She said okay, she would, but then she never did.

Roby became our fifth cat. She came from the back road. My mom, Edward, and I were walking to Mr. Miller's to watch the horses when I heard a cry. It came from a tiny gray and white kitten hiding in the honeysuckle along the fencerow. Someone had probably dropped her there. I said that we had to take her home; Mom sighed, shook her head, and said, "Oh, dear." Roby was very hungry and tired. For many days after I got her home, she ate and slept and ate and slept and ate and slept. It was Mom who named her Roby, after a cat she had when she was little.

I have written each cat's story for school for different teachers. Everybody is tired of hearing about the cats.

Smokey had lain down on my stomach and now he was asleep. I squinted my eyes as tightly shut as Smokey's and thought about the summer. Last summer I had taken swimming lessons and like every summer I can remember, I had gone to the beach in Nags Head, North Carolina. I had gone to Mr. Miller's farm and watched Mr. Miller's horses, too. They are old, too old to ride he says, so my friend Edward and I had watched them eat, and I had pretended that I had a horse of my own.

I knew I would go the the beach this summer, but I fell asleep wondering what else I would do.

2. Poor, Sad Dog

The radio from the kitchen woke me. Mom was up, and Mr. Wood's truck hadn't come back. I didn't want to go into the house. Mom probably already had a list of spring cleaning things that I would have to help with. My mom likes to make lists.

I yawned and stretched and rubbed my eyes and got up and went into the house because I couldn't put it off forever. Mom was drinking hot tea and writing something on a piece of paper. It looked like a list to me.

"Spring cleaning?" I asked.

Mom laughed. "You don't sound too thrilled."

"I *hate* spring cleaning," I said.

"Isn't 'hate' kind of a strong word?"

"Not for spring cleaning."

"I guess," Mom suggested, "we could trade.

I think I hate yard and garden work as much as you hate spring cleaning."

"Trade?"

"If I don't have to pull weeds, you don't have to dust and wash windows."

"I do the outside work?"

"Except for the mowing. Your dad will have to mow."

"And you do the inside work?"

"Yes . . . except for your room. You have to clean out your closet and under the bed and your dresser drawers and the closet." Mom paused to put jelly on a biscuit. "Oh, and your desk. You'd have to do your desk."

Roby and Pinkie followed me to the garden and watched me pull weeds and hoe around the plants. I should have thought of trading myself. Last summer, Mom had complained a lot every time we had to work in the garden or help Dad in the yard.

I was still in the garden pulling weeds when my friend Edward parked his bike in the driveway. "Want to take swimming lessons?" he asked as he crossed the lawn. "My mom said she'd take us. They start week after next. Every day from nine to ten in the morning."

We had taken lessons last summer, and we both had passed Beginners. "Sure," I answered. "But I want to take Beginners again. You think they'd let me?"

"You could ask."

I bent over and pulled tiny weeds from around a tomato plant. I was hoping Edward wouldn't ask me why I wanted to take Beginners again. I didn't mind if he knew, but I didn't want to say why out loud.

"You don't want to dive off the board, do you? Intermediates have to dive off the board."

I looked up at Edward. Hearing him say it was almost as bad as saying it myself. "Don't tell anybody," I said. I bent over another tomato plant, feeling ashamed that I was afraid.

"No problem," Edward answered with a shrug. "Well, I've got to call to register us today. The classes will get full. Are you in or not?"

"Yes," I answered. "If Mom says yes." I carried a handful of weeds to the end of the row and tossed them onto the pile that I had made there.

Edward followed me into the house. Mom was on the phone talking to Aunt Debbie. I wrote on the message pad: "Swimming lessons? Yes or No" and handed Mom the note and pen. She circled "Yes" and smiled at Edward. My mom likes Edward. He's an A student. I'm an A, B, C student. I think she wishes I were more like him.

"I want you to meet someone," I said when we were back outside. "Come on."

Booford was asleep near the door of his house, but he hopped to his feet and barked crazily when we crossed the road. Edward stopped at the edge of the yard. "Booford?" he said. "An ugly name for an ugly dog."

Sometimes Edward is too honest. "He's not ugly," I said. I cupped Booford's face between my hands and kissed him on the forehead.

"Are you crazy?" Edward asked. "Can't you read? 'Beware of Dog.' " He stepped backward onto the road, frowning.

"That sign is a fake. This dog is nice. Mr. Wood is mean."

"Mr. Wood?" Edward questioned.

"The man who lives here," I answered. "The man who just moved in. He's big and mean and I bet he's never nice to Booford. All he does is yell at him."

"Is Mr. Wood home?" Edward asked as he glanced toward the house.

"No."

Edward looked toward the highway. "Does this Mr. Wood mind if you pet his dog?" he asked.

"Probably."

"Let's get out of here," Edward said, and he turned and crossed the road.

"Don't listen to Edward," I whispered in Boo's ear. "You are a beautiful dog." Boo wagged his tail and jumped up and put his paws around my waist.

Edward stopped in my front yard to pet Hairy. Then he got on his bike and rode away without another word. I am used to Edward doing that. Sometimes he doesn't explain. He just does things.

I sat in the grass. Booford put his head on my lap. "Boo," I said, "I don't have a dog. Just cats. I told you that already, didn't I? Anyway, Mom says cats are enough. I'll have to ask Aunt Debbie to bring her dog Sandy over to play with you. Sometimes I take Sandy for walks. I bet you'd like to go for a walk." Booford's eyes were shut. I lifted one of his ears. "I have to go," I said. "Be good."

Boo barked and bounced up and down when I left.

Mr. Wood was gone all day. I pulled weeds and watched for him. It was almost seven when his truck turned into the driveway.

He didn't play with Booford that evening. He didn't walk Booford that evening. He didn't talk to him. I'm a good hearer. I can hear noises far away, so I know Mr. Wood just walked right by a jumping-up-and-down-and-barking-madly dog.

That evening I told my dad we had to do something about that poor, sad old dog.

Every morning all week long I watched Booford. Every morning was the same. Before Mr. Wood left his house in his blue pickup truck, he gave Booford fresh water and food. Booford jumped up and down and barked, but when Mr. Wood yelled "Shut up, dog!" he dropped to the ground and was quiet.

On Friday, after Mr. Wood had gone, Booford walked to the end of his chain and began circling the tree where he was tied. He walked around and around and around. After he had made about ten circles, I yelled, "Booford, you'll get dizzy." He stopped and barked at me and then started circling again. Around and around and around. Around and around and around. I was getting dizzy watching him.

At last, Booford had to stop because his chain was too short for him to walk any farther. As he walked, he had wrapped his chain around the tree. But Booford knew what to do. He turned around and went in the opposite direction until the chain was unwrapped. Booford circled the tree all morning long.

In the afternoon, he tried something new. He dug two holes under the tree. I stopped pulling weeds from the garden and raced across the road. "Silly dog," I said to Booford. "Your master will be angry. You must *not* dig holes. No more holes," I repeated firmly, pointing at them and shaking my head no.

I scraped the soil back into the holes with my hands and placed small chunks of grass on top. I didn't do a very good job. The grass clods broke apart, and dirt sifted down into the grass around the holes.

When I finished doing the best I could, I stood up and dusted the dirt from my knees. Booford put his paws around my waist and licked my nose.

"I have to go," I said and backed out of his reach. He lay down then on his side, but he didn't close his eyes. He just lay there breathing, staring at nothing. "You're bored, aren't you?" I asked him. "You want to play or go for a walk." His skinny tail flopped against the ground and he rolled over onto his back. I patted his smooth, round tummy.

As I stepped away from him, he leaped to his feet and started barking again. Gently, I stroked his head, down his nose, and around his eyes and ears. He stopped barking. "Booford," I whispered, "I'll help you." A drop of water slipped out of one of his eyes. "Have you got a bug or some dirt in your eye, Boo, or is that a tear?" I asked him.

I walked away and he started barking. He

barked until I sat down on the top of the porch steps. In five seconds, he had flung the dirt back out of both holes. He had just finished slinging dirt and dust when Mr. Wood drove into the driveway. I put my hands over my ears.

Mr. Wood hopped from his truck and shouted, "Hey, you dumb dog, cut that out! You're making a mess of this yard!" At once Boo lay down in one of the holes, and Mr. Wood disappeared into the house. I waited to see if Mr. Wood would come back out with a fly swatter or something to beat the dog with. But he didn't.

When Dad came home, I was sitting on the front porch steps again and Boo was lying in a hole.

"Hayley," he asked, "what's wrong?" He pulled my braids forward and tied them under my chin.

"Nothing . . . much."

"Enough of a much to make you sad," Dad said, and he sat down beside me on the steps. "Are you feeling okay?"

"Yes."

"Did a cat get killed?"

"No."

"You found another stray and don't want to tell me?"

"No."

"You found *two* strays and don't want to tell me."

I laughed.

"That's better," Dad said. "Now, what in the world is your 'nothing much'?"

"Booford," I said, and I pointed across the street.

Daddy looked in that direction. " 'Beware of Dog,' " he read aloud.

"It should say 'Beware of Man,' " I told him. "That dog is friendly and loving and kind. Mr. Wood is mean. 'Beware of Mr. Wood' is what it should say."

"Did Mr. Wood mistreat the dog? Beat him or something?"

"No, but he yelled at him and he didn't pet him and he didn't pay any attention to him, and he doesn't take him for walks, and Booford is so tired of being tied to that tree."

"Hayley, dogs have to be tied. There's a county law. Besides, if he were loose, he might get hit by a car. Anyway, Mr. Wood just moved in. Give the man a chance. He'll probably walk Booford this weekend. Tomorrow or Sunday, I bet." Daddy got up from the steps. "Now let's go eat supper," he said. He looked over toward Booford again. " 'Beware of Dog,' " he repeated. "I wonder why he put that sign up if the dog isn't mean."

"Maybe to keep away children," I said. "I don't think he likes children."

Daddy looked serious. "We don't know Mr. Wood," he said. "We really don't. You'd better not go over there, at least not until I have a chance to talk to the man."

"Oh, Dad, I don't go over there when Mr. Wood is home. I only go when he's gone. He doesn't even know I visit Booford. That poor dog will go crazy if somebody doesn't talk to him."

"I doubt that," Dad said.

3. Herkimer

It was ten-thirty Saturday morning. I sat on the front porch swing with Hairy and Pinkie and waited for Edward, who was late. He was probably doing some science experiment or reading about black holes or taking something apart.

For the first time ever, my mom was letting Edward and me walk to Mr. Miller's farm by ourselves. The farm was two miles from my house. Mr. Miller raised Black Angus cattle and he had two old horses, four dogs, and a lot of cats; he didn't know how many. He fed the cats every day, but he didn't count them. I had told him he should get the mother cats spayed so they wouldn't keep having kittens, but he never had. Some of the cats were wild, and he couldn't even touch them.

Edward liked Mr. Miller's horses and, of

course, he liked Hairy, but he isn't really the crazy kind of animal lover that I am. Still, he always listened to Mr. Miller's animal stories and to mine. I guess he listened because he was a polite person, and also because I always listened to his rocket stories and his computer stories.

Booford came from inside his doghouse and looked in my direction. Then he started running back and forth and barking. He had seen Edward walking down the road.

"I want to take Boo along," I said when Edward reached the yard.

"Who?"

Booford barked.

"Oh, the dog. Well, you go ask. I'm not knocking on his door. Mom and I took Mr. Wood some cupcakes yesterday. He said he didn't like cupcakes. He practically shut the door in our faces. Even if he didn't like cupcakes, he should have said thank you. And he could have been a lot more polite."

"Okay," I said, "I'll ask." Boo barked loudly when I started up the sidewalk.

"Shut up, dog!" a deep voice yelled from inside the house. "Shut up, NOW!"

I backed a few steps down the walk and then turned and ran to catch up with Edward. Hairy was following him, trotting along in the grass near the fence. I couldn't let him follow us. I scooped him up quickly, carried his wiggly, trying-to-escape body to the house, put him on the back porch, and ran to catch up with Edward again. Booford barked and barked, and once again I heard Mr. Wood's booming voice.

Edward and I crossed over two hills, and my house disappeared, and Boo's bark faded. We passed dairy cows who paused and lifted their heads to watch us.

"He's not walking him then," Edward finally said. It was more of a comment than a question.

"Are you kidding! He never even says 'Hi, Boo.' "

"The dog does have food and water, doesn't he?"

"Yes. Dad always asks me the same thing."

We stopped at the little bridge, startling two frogs who plopped into the stream.

"Swimming lessons start next week," Edward said.

"I know."

Edward pushed tiny pieces of gravel from the roadside into the water.

"Don't," I said. "You might hit a fish."

Edward looked at me and shook his head. "Sometimes," he said, "you're ridiculous."

We reached the big bridge, the halfway point, fifteen minutes later. From there we left the paved road and continued on a small, dirt road that ran parallel to Smith Creek.

"I want to check the stone fence," Edward said.

A Civil War battle had been fought around the stone fence. All winter long, when our school bus passed the wall, Edward had talked about searching for Civil War things near the fence.

Honeysuckle and other vines almost covered the stones. "This looks like a good place for snakes," I said. I wouldn't hurt a snake, but I

didn't want to find one. Snakes make me feel creepy. I walked ahead, leaving Edward alone to search.

Sunlight filtered through huge, old trees, making scattered patches of light on the dirt road. Carefully, I tramped through tall grass and jumped down a small bank to the edge of the creek. Clear water splashed and gurgled and bubbled over rocks before flowing into a wider, smooth current. I sat on a big rock and pretended Boo was along, splashing around, spraying me with water when he shook his body. I started smiling, thinking about it.

"Hey, Hayley! Hey, Hayley!" Edward shouted. "Come here!" I bounded up the bank and raced down the road.

In the palm of Edward's hand lay a shiny, pointed rock.

"Indians made this?" I asked.

"Yep." Edward beamed.

I touched the point. "And they shot animals?"

"Probably small game—rabbits and squirrels." Edward closed his hand gently. "I'm going to start a collection," he announced. Edward collects everything: stamps and coins and weather facts and pictures of rockets.

I don't care about those things, but Indian arrowheads are different. "I'll help," I offered.

We set off once again for the farm. Mr. Miller was in the barn unloading hay when we arrived. Danny, a high school senior hired by Mr. Miller to help him with the summer farm work, stood on the back of a wagon, throwing bales of hay into a noisy electric elevator. Mr. Miller was high in the barn picking up and stacking the bales as they dropped from the elevator onto the floor of the haymow. He picked up a bale, and then he disappeared as he moved to the back of the mow to stack the hay.

"Can we help?" I shouted when Mr. Miller came into view again.

"Come on up . . . carefully," he shouted back. He must have guessed what I asked because he couldn't have heard me above the noise of the clanging elevator. Edward followed me up the ladder.

The bales were too heavy for me or Edward to lift, though I almost could. I grabbed a bale of hay by the twine that held it together and pulled and rolled it to the back of the mow. Back and forth we went, lugging bales of hay. I felt beads of perspiration on my forehead, and soon my back felt wet and my shirt was sticking to my skin. Edward's face was red, and I supposed that mine was, too. The bales were heavy and the temperature that high up in the barn on a June day must have been about eighty-five degrees.

In half an hour we had finished. Danny cut the elevator off, and we climbed down the ladder. Danny left for home, and Mr. Miller went to the house to get us all some iced tea and peanut butter crackers.

While we were sitting on the wagon waiting, Edward touched my arm and pointed. A tiny gray kitten was standing on three legs in the doorway of the barn. Then the mother cat and two other kittens appeared. They charged past the gray kitten and noisily crunched on the dry food that was in a dish against the wall. The kitten limped across the barn, dragging her lame back leg on the wooden floor. She didn't see us, and when she came to the wagon, she stopped right under our dangling feet.

The moment I saw the kitten and realized that she was hurt, I knew that some way, somehow, I just had to help her. I thought, what will Mom say? but I pushed that thought away, jumped from the wagon, and scrambled to grab for the kitten. The kitten hunched her back and hissed, giving me a second to close my fingers tightly on the scruff of her neck. Quickly, I lifted her from the barn floor, and then I felt teeth and claws dig into my arm, and I screamed and

slung her away. She hit the stack of hay, bounced up, and darted on her three good legs behind some pipes and farm equipment parts that were piled in the corner.

Edward hopped from the wagon and ran past me to the corner of the barn. He peered between pipes and engine parts. "I don't see her," he said. "I'm afraid to move anything. I could make the whole mess of stuff fall down on top of the cat."

Mr. Miller came back then with three glasses of iced tea and a plate of peanut butter crackers. "There's a kitten that's hurt, Mr. Miller," I told him. "Bad, I think. We have to catch her."

"I know," he said handing me a glass of tea. "But I can't catch her. I've tried. She can run as fast on three legs as the others run on four."

"She needs to go to the vet."

"I know, but I have to catch her first."

I thought about her dragging that leg over rocks and thistles in the fields. "I tried to catch her," I said. "I missed." I felt tears in my throat. I hate crying in front of people. I swallowed hard and gulped some tea. "I grabbed for her and she bit me and I threw her down. I bet I broke her ribs." I held up my arm. There were two scratches and a few tiny holes made by tiny teeth.

"Young lady," Mr. Miller said firmly, "that needs to be washed with hot, soapy water." He grasped my wrist and turned my forearm so that he could see the wounds. "You might need a penicillin shot. And is your tetanus up to date?"

"I don't know. I'll be okay. Don't worry about it."

"I'll have to talk to your mother," he said. "But"—he paused and smiled at me—"but," he repeated, "I guess we could try to get that little cat first. I've been wanting to do something about her.

"Edward, you go down the steps in the back and see if you can find my live trap. I'll get some sardines, and if we're lucky, we'll catch that little cat in just a few minutes."

Edward disappeared down the steps and was back up very quickly carrying a long metal-and-wire box. I sat on the wagon, trying to act as if my arm didn't hurt.

By the time Mr. Miller returned with an open can of sardines, three paper towels, and a fork, the mother and other kittens had finished eating and left the barn. The gray kitten was still hiding in the corner.

Mr. Miller carefully folded the towels and placed some bits of sardines on each one. He set the trap near the dry cat food dish. He placed one towel near the trap, one just inside the open door, and the other in the back of the trap. "When the kitten reaches for the food in the back," he said, "she'll probably tramp on this plate and . . ." He reached inside the trap and gently pushed on a piece of aluminum in the middle of the wire floor. The door of the trap banged shut so suddenly that I jumped. "And the door closes and we have one cat, caught," he finished. "Let's go outside."

We went out the barn door and wandered partway down the driveway toward the house. We had been there barely one minute when there was a bang. "That's it," said Mr. Miller. "Either she's caught or she just tripped the trap." I ran back up the road to the barn.

The injured kitten darted madly back and forth and banged her head against the door and sides of the trap, trying desperately to escape. I spoke softly to her, but she was too frantic and scared to hear me.

Mr. Miller drove the kitten, Edward, and me to Dr. Rhodes's office, where we left the kitten. Then he drove me home. Mom called the doctor; he said my tetanus shot was still good and that antibiotic cream should be put on my cat bites and scratches. If my arm was red on Monday, I had to go see him.

I couldn't go to sleep Saturday night for a

long time. I kept thinking about the gray kitten. I felt really happy that we had caught her but I felt worried, too, because she was so scared of people. I didn't know how the vet could do anything with such a frightened cat. I hoped kittens couldn't die from heart attacks caused by being afraid. Somehow, it seemed to me that Saturday had lasted about two days.

My arm hurt and felt hot. I didn't tell Mom but she knew. I pretended to be asleep when she came to my bedroom with an ice pack and placed it gently on my forearm. That felt cool and then I really did fall asleep.

*

Sunday evening, Mom, Dad, and I were eating watermelon in the backyard when Mr. Miller parked his truck in the driveway. He had a cat carrier with him.

"I need a favor," he said. He took off his cap; his gray hair was sticking out from his head. "I need somebody to keep this little creature in a clean, dry place until her wound heals. She had to have that leg amputated, and Dr. Rhodes said if I let her go in the barn she could get an infection and die. Louise said if I let a cat loose in the house, *I'll* die, because she'll kill me."

It seemed strange, but a good strange, to see

a big man with gray hair sticking out sideways pleading for a little gray kitten.

Dad and I glanced at each other, and I knew it was okay with him. Mom looked at Dad. Mr. Miller scratched his head and put his hat back on.

"We'll keep her," Mom said, "for six weeks. Then you can put her back in the barn. And, Hayley Larken, the cat needs to stay in the basement."

"But the basement is damp and dark and . . ."

"Okay . . . all right . . . in your room . . . but if she doesn't use the litter box, it's to the basement."

Mr. Miller brought the carrier to my bedroom. I found a cardboard box and filled it with litter and got the kitten some water and some food. Mom put everything on newspapers and old place mats.

"Six weeks," she repeated to Mr. Miller.

Dad got down on his hands and knees and peered inside the carrier. The kitten cowered in the back with her face under a blanket. "Did you name her?" Dad asked.

"Herkimer," I said, without even really thinking about it much. "Herkimer."

Sometime that evening or night, Herkimer

left the carrier and hid under my bed. That's where she was at ten o'clock when I came back upstairs. I lay on my stomach and shifted boxes under the bed, but she moved from side to side so that I couldn't even get a good look at her.

I had to keep the bedroom door shut, which caused a problem because Smokey likes to sleep with me. The very first night that Herkie was there, Smokey sat outside my room scratching and scratching on the closed door. Several times I got up and went out into the hallway to hold him. Twice I took him downstairs and put him on the sofa, but both times he beat me back up the stairs. Cats never stay where you put them. I think they must have a rule about that. Finally, when my clock said 2:00 A.M., the scratching stopped.

At breakfast the next morning, Dad said that sometime in the night Smokey had hopped up onto the bed with Mom and him and had settled down between them on the pillows and fallen asleep.

"Did he purr?" I asked, feeling a little guilty.

"Loud and clear," Dad said, "just like old times. Before you were born, he always used to sleep with us, you know."

That day, I tried to get close enough to Herkie to see her stitches because I was worried about her shoulder—where the leg had been removed—getting infected. But I couldn't get anywhere near her. I called Dr. Rhodes. He told me that he had given Herkimer a long-acting injection to fight against infection and that her stitches would dissolve on their own. He told me not to worry about her unless she stopped eating. But she ate well, and she used her litter box, which was a very good thing because—I didn't tell Mom—there was no way I could have caught her to put her in the basement if she hadn't.

4. Swimming Lessons

The water was cold, but as I bobbed up and down, under and out of the six-foot-deep water, blowing bubbles and kicking, I warmed up. The swimming teacher made us bob every day first thing to get accustomed to the cool water and to practice for our survival test. I liked to bob. I was good at it.

When I popped out of the water, I could see mothers sitting on the observatory roof of the park building, waiting for the lessons to end. Though I couldn't pick her out in the few seconds I was above water during each bob, I knew Edward's mother was there, watching us. Edward wasn't beside me. He usually stayed near the shallow end; he liked being able to touch the bottom of the pool.

Edward and I were both in Advanced Beginners, a new class created for ten of us who were not ready for Intermediate, but who had passed Beginners.

The Intermediate lessons finished right before our class started. On the second day of lessons, just as I had guessed, Intermediates were diving from the board. We dived on the second day, too, but from the side of the pool. All I had to do was stand with straight legs and bend over to touch my toes until I fell headfirst into the water. I was really glad not to be an Intermediate.

"Laps, laps," shouted Mrs. Shelly, our teacher, walking down the side of the pool and clapping her hands. I swam to the side and held on. Mrs. Shelly reviewed the arm movements for the American Crawl. "Two laps," she ordered. "And, remember, a lap is over and back."

Last year the American Crawl had made me tired very easily; this year I swam two laps without feeling tired at all.

Next came swimming on our backs. All we had to do was flutter kick across the pool—no arm movements. Partners were to watch each other. Edward and I were partners.

The teacher moved us to the middle, where Edward could touch the bottom but I couldn't. I told him to go first. He pushed off the side of the pool and kicked hard toward the opposite side; then, halfway across, he turned toward the deep end. I yelled but he didn't hear me. His eyes shut, he merrily kicked and kicked his way into deeper and deeper water. Mrs. Shelly, who was leaning over the edge of the pool talking to another student, didn't see him.

He'll be fine, I told myself. He'll just bump his head on the pool side. And that is what he did. In about thirty seconds, he bumped into the side at the deep end of the pool; he turned, looked surprised, disappeared under the water, came up, and grabbed the edge.

Edward's mom got to the pool's edge just as Edward grabbed hold.

"Let's go," she said. "That's it."

Edward got out of the water. His mom hung his towel around him and pulled on his arm. He jerked away and let the towel drop to the pavement. "What's the matter?" he demanded.

Mrs. Zirkle was almost crying. "You could have drowned," she said, with a quiver in her voice. Edward looked at the ground. His face went from white to red. Mrs. Zirkle turned and left, and Edward followed her out of the pool area. No one said a word.

I felt embarrassed for Edward and mad at myself. I should have jumped into the pool and tried to stop him. I should have done something.

I looked at Mrs. Shelly, wishing she could fix things. She bit her lower lip. "Everyone into the pool," she ordered. "We have fifteen minutes left. Advanced Beginners, repeat your back swimming."

After the lesson was over, I called Mom to pick me up. Edward was on the front porch when I got home. I sat on the top step in my wet bathing suit, wishing my dad was there to talk to Edward. I hoped I could say the right thing, the way he would. "Are you coming back to swimming?" I asked.

Edward didn't answer.

"Your mom looked dumb today," I said. "Not you. You were swimming in the deep end, you know."

Edward laughed. "I know," he said. "And it was great!"

"Nobody thought you were dumb. Your mom, maybe. But not you."

"My mom is my mom," Edward said and shrugged his shoulders. "The whole world knows that. I quit trying to change her three years ago. She doesn't really embarrass me much anymore. Makes me angry, sometimes. Then, I think about it and I can't stay mad."

He let out a deep breath. "She's just trying to be Mom *and* Dad, you know."

"I know," I said. Edward's mom and dad were divorced when Edward was four. I barely remembered Edward's dad. I don't think Edward remembered him very well or even missed him very much, except when his mom treated him like a baby and acted like such a worrywart.

"Forget it. I'll just be in Advanced Beginners again next year," he said.

"Maybe my dad could talk to her. He's very good at talking."

"No . . . it's okay. Just forget it."

"How about Mrs. Shelly? She could call your mom."

"Hayley, look at me. Look at me!"

I turned to face Edward.

"F-O-R-G-E-T I-T," he spelled.

"Okay," I mumbled. "Okay." I wished he would let me try. I really wanted to help.

"I've got other stuff to do anyway. The library has three new rocket books, and I've got to go back to the stone fence on the back road."

A white truck stopped in front of Mr. Wood's house. Booford barked and pranced and jumped around. "That's Dr. Rhodes's truck," I told Edward as I bounded down the stairs and crossed the back road.

Dr. Rhodes had opened one of the compartments on the back of his pickup truck. He was looking for medicine or something. The whole back of Dr. Rhodes's truck looked like a big toolbox. He had to carry medical tools and equipment and medicines with him to farms. One part was like a refrigerator.

Boo had stopped barking and stood watching us, his tail wagging.

"Hey, Hayley," Dr. Rhodes said. "How are you? How are the cats?"

"Fine," I said. "What are you doing here?"

"I've been hired to vaccinate Mr. Wood's dog. He stopped in and set it up with Pat. I told him there would be a farm call charge, and he could bring the dog in during Saturday office hours. But he said he didn't want to haul the dog in his truck."

"I'm not surprised at anything mean that man says."

"Here, hold these, please." Dr. Rhodes handed me two bottles that held the vaccines. "One's for rabies and one's for parvo." Then he opened another door and got a syringe. I liked watching Dr. Rhodes, but I didn't like seeing the needle. I hoped Booford wouldn't mind the shots. "Do you know Mr. Wood?" Dr. Rhodes asked.

"Not really. Not very well. I know he doesn't like children, and I don't think he likes Booford."

"Didn't he just move here?" Dr. Rhodes questioned. He pulled the pink cover from the needle with his teeth and took one of the bottles from me. He drew the liquid into the syringe.

"About two weeks ago," I answered.

"Come and hold the dog for me, will you?"

"Sure," I said.

Boo pranced back and forth. I held his collar and tried to make him stand still. I don't think he felt either shot.

While I was helping Dr. Rhodes, Edward left.

That night, I told Dad about Booford's shots and what happened at swimming lessons. Dad said he'd take Edward and me to the pool as soon as he could. I was glad because I thought Edward should go in deep water again soon. I thought his mind might remember the bad part—the going under—and forget the good part—swimming half the length of the pool, mostly in water over his head.

On Sunday, Dad took us swimming after church. Edward swam the length of the pool on his back with my Dad swimming beside him, and he dived off the board with Dad there to swim beside him to the edge. He went up high and came down with just a tiny splash. I was amazed at the neatness of his dive. Edward is pudgy and he wears glasses, and he has never been good at any other sport. I am usually the one who's good at athletics. It took about twenty practice dives from the pool ledge, with my dad there making me laugh, before I finally did two dives from the board. I felt proud of myself and even more proud of Edward. I told him to tell his mom about the diving and the deep water, but I didn't think he would.

5. Plan A and Plan B

I was right. I wished Dr. Rhodes and my dad were right, but they were wrong and I was right. Not once during June, that I knew of, did Mr. Wood take Booford for a walk or play with him or let him loose to run. Every day was the same. Booford walked around the tree, dug holes, barked at me, and slept. Mostly, though, he just lay there—looking away at nothing. I thought maybe he was daydreaming about running across fields or up big, green hills. I thought, too, suppose he never, ever got walked—not even once.

And then I thought, hey you dummy, this is a dog. This is not a horse. He probably doesn't care that much about running anyway.

Still, every day when Dad came home from work I would say, "We've got to do something about that poor, sad old dog."

And Dad would say, "That poor, sad old dog has plenty of food, fresh water, and a dog-house. And you for a friend."

On the very last Sunday in June, I decided that if I *was* Booford's friend, I had to do something to help him. One whole month with no walks was awful to think about. I marched across the street to Mr. Wood's house. It was time for Plan A. I was going to say, "Sir, your dog digs holes, barks, and walks in circles because he is bored. If you don't take him for a walk, I'm going to call the Humane Society."

Mr. Wood's front door stood open, and through the screen door I could see into the living room. Mr. Wood was asleep in a huge, green chair. On television some cowboys were chasing train robbers. Mr. Wood wore blue jeans and a brown short sleeve shirt. On both arms there were bluish-purple designs and letters. There was a heart with an arrow through the center on one arm, and on the other arm there were some letters, but I couldn't read the word the letters spelled. A smelly cigar burned in an ashtray which was on the floor beside a pair of pointed-toe cowboy boots. Sunday comics were scattered around the room.

A car drove by and Booford started barking. Mr. Wood moved around and mumbled something. I thought he was waking up. I stumbled backward, turned, tripped over a shoelace, and fell on the sidewalk. Of course, Booford barked and barked at me. That did wake Mr. Wood, who got to the door of his house before I could get up.

"Kid, you okay?" he asked, opening the screen door.

"I'm okay," I answered and got to my feet. Then I don't know why but my tongue kept going. "My mom sent me over to see if you want some tomatoes," I lied. "We have lots of tomatoes. It's really early to have tomatoes. My dad always gives the first ripe tomato to me and, most years, that doesn't happen until the middle of July. We plant our garden late. Other people have tomatoes sooner than us." I have always talked too much when I'm nervous.

Mr. Wood didn't say a word; he just stared at me.

"Your knee is bleeding," he finally said. "Wait here."

He disappeared inside the house. Then he returned with a wet washcloth and iodine and knelt in the grass to wash my knee. When the warm washcloth touched my skin, I jumped a little, and he jerked the washcloth away. "Sorry," he mumbled. Then, very, very gently, he pressed the cloth against the scrape once again. "I don't think this will burn," he said before he dabbed on the iodine.

"It doesn't," I said. He and I were both looking at my knee, not at each other's faces. He didn't really get my knee clean, and he put on a lot more iodine than necessary, but I didn't say anything.

When he put the top back on the iodine bottle, I asked again, "Well, did you want any tomatoes?"

"I don't like tomatoes," he said slowly. He stood and so did I. Boy, was he tall. When I looked straight ahead, I saw myself in the middle of his shiny belt buckle.

"I do," I said quietly and raised my eyes to meet his. "I love tomatoes." He was silent. "Bye," I said. My face felt hot.

I raced home and up the steps and into the living room. From behind the curtains, I peeped out the front window and saw Mr. Wood staring at the house.

Mom was lying on the sofa, half-watching the same western as Mr. Wood and half-sleeping. "What in the world are you doing?" she asked. "Spying on somebody?"

"Watching Mr. Wood," I answered. "He's staring at our house."

"Why is Mr. Wood staring at our house? And what happened to your knee?"

"Oh, that's iodine," I answered. "I fell down on Mr. Wood's sidewalk." I let the curtain drop into place. "He doesn't like tomatoes," I added.

"I know," she answered. "I offered him some this morning. He's allergic to them. He gets red spots if he eats them."

"Oh," I mumbled. My face felt hot again.

"So, why is Mr. Wood staring at our house?" Mom asked once more.

"He's not anymore," I said. "He just went inside." I sat down on the rocking chair and pushed myself back and forth.

I tried to watch the movie, but I couldn't really pay attention. I was thinking about Mr. Wood. "Mr. Wood was watching this same movie," I said. "But he was asleep, too." Mom had closed her eyes again.

"Did you wake him up?" Mom mumbled.

"No, but Booford did." I rocked back and forth and back and forth. "Mom," I said, "Mr. Wood seems kind of lonely, don't you think?"

"Oh, I don't know. He seemed all right this morning."

The rocking chair made creaking noises as I rocked back and forth. The creaking sounded lonely, too.

"Why," Mom asked after I thought for sure that she was asleep, "do you think he's lonely?"

"I don't know. He doesn't talk much. Nobody visits him, and I just think he looks lonely."

"Hmm," Mom mumbled. I waited for her to say more, but she really was asleep.

I went up to my room and tried again to make friends with Herkimer, but she wouldn't come out from under the bed. Lying flat on my stomach with my arm stretched to the limit, I barely managed to touch her back. She jumped, darted across the room, slid sideways on the hardwood floor, and scooted under the dresser.

Plan A, Talk to Mr. Wood, had failed. Plan B, Give Mr. Wood a Hint, was next.

*

The next afternoon, I found the cat collar and leash in the porch cabinet. Last summer I had spent hours and hours trying to train Smokey to go for walks. But Smokey didn't like the collar. He had pawed at it and gone in circles trying to get it off. I had put it in the cabinet and that is where it had stayed until now.

Without the slightest trouble, I put the collar on Hairy and then hooked the leash to the collar. When I knew it was almost time for Mr.

Wood to come home from work, I carried Hairy to the front yard. As soon as I saw Mr. Wood's truck turn onto our road from Route 11, I started walking and pulled on the leash for Hairy to follow. I was hoping that if Mr. Wood saw me walking Hairy, he would think about walking Booford.

Unfortunately, Hairy didn't go along with my plan. He wouldn't move. I pulled, and all that happened was that I dragged Hairy through the grass. As Mr. Wood drove past us, Hairy twisted his head out of the collar and darted across the pavement and straight up the tree where Booford was tied.

Booford bounced up and down on all fours and barked happily. Hairy climbed higher and higher up the tree.

Mr. Wood turned into his driveway, got out of his truck, and leaned against it. He took a cigar from his pocket and lit it. I stood beside him and peered up the tree. Between Booford's loud barks I asked him, "What should we do?"

"Nothing," he muttered around the cigar.

"But . . . Hairy . . . my cat?"

"He'll come down," he said and smacked at a fly that was on his arm, sitting on the purple writing, right on the *R*, the first letter in the word *Ruby*. "It seems to me like this black cat is the same black cat who comes over here and sits on my truck every night."

"Hairy always was a friendly cat," I said. "I guess he comes over to see Booford."

"The next time you talk to Hairy, kid, you tell him that I said to stay off my truck. Every day it's the same. Cat prints on the hood. Cat prints up the windshield. Cat prints across the top." He chewed his cigar and rolled it around in his mouth. I bit my lip.

"He'll come down later," Mr. Wood said. He

trudged up the walk and into the house, pulling the front door shut with a bang.

I wandered home and sat on the porch steps. Plan B had failed. At least, I thought, Booford's not bored tonight. He was still barking wildly at Hairy.

Mom came outside and sat beside me on the step. "What has Booford treed?" she asked.

"Hairy." I sighed.

"Your Hairy?"

"My Hairy. Mr. Wood said he'll come down later."

"I'm sure he will. If he doesn't your dad will get him."

"Mr. Wood is never going to walk that dog," I said, and it made me sad and mad all over again to say it. "It is so dumb," I said. "All the man has to do is get a leash and hook it to his collar and go."

"Hayley, Hayley," Mom said softly and touched my knee. "You get so serious sometimes! Anne, my friend all through elementary school, never walked her dog. She had a little beagle named Martha that she kept tied at a doghouse in the back yard."

"She never let her loose to play?"

"No."

"That's awful."

"I guess the only time Martha was loose was when Anne took her to the veterinarian. Oh, I do remember one time she got loose. I guess we were in high school then. I helped Anne find her."

"Did you tell Anne she should walk her dog?"

"No."

"Maybe you should have."

"It's not that Anne mistreated the dog. She just didn't walk her.

"That *is* mistreating her," I said. Mom didn't answer. "How long did Martha live?" I asked.

"Seventeen years."

"That's pretty old for a dog. Are you sure?"

"Positive."

"Seventeen years and no walks," I said aloud.

"Not that I know of."

"Oh, Mom, don't tell me any more. It's too sad."

"Hayley, the point is I don't think Martha was that sad. She was never loose except that one time she escaped, so I guess she didn't know what she was missing. She never seemed sad to me." Mom smiled. "So, cheer up," she added.

I smiled back, sort of, but inside I didn't feel very cheery. I was thinking, Mom, you are wrong, wrong, wrong. You don't know animals like I do. But I didn't say anything.

"Hairy's down," Mom said suddenly.

Hairy ran across the road and scooted up a tree in our yard. Boo's barking changed to a whimper as he watched Hairy escape.

That night I lay awake for a long time thinking about Booford and about Martha and about the things Mom had said. I knew my mom was saying Boo wasn't the only dog in the world who wasn't walked. That was true. She was saying maybe Booford and other tied-up, never-walked dogs aren't really sad. That was wrong. Booford, I was sure, was very sad and very, very bored. And probably so was Martha, but Mom just didn't know it. And Mom was saying, Hayley, just forget it. You can't fix it so just forget it. She was right—I couldn't fix it. But I couldn't forget it either.

"God bless Booford," I whispered, "and Mom and Dad and all the cats and Edward and Herkimer." Finally, I fell asleep, but then I dreamed about Booford. I dreamed that he was running loose and his ears were flying straight back in the wind. He was barking and I was laughing. I woke up suddenly and I could hear Booford barking. I looked out my window, but he wasn't running loose. He was chained to his doghouse and was walking around and around and around and barking and barking.

I left my room, closing the door behind me. I tiptoed down the stairs in the dark. I quietly unlocked the front door and slipped outside. The moon was full and made the night very light. There were no lights on in any of the houses, just the outdoor light from the Zirkles' garage. The grass was already wet from dew. I hurried across the yard and across the back road to Boo's doghouse. He rushed to meet me. He jumped up and placed his paws around my waist and held on to me. He wagged from his tail to his ears. His whole body danced. I scratched his ears and under his chin.

My hands felt the chain that hooked to his collar. I could unhook that chain very easily, I thought. I could set Boo free. He could run loose, and his ears would fly in the wind.

Just then, I heard a car pass by on Route 11. Suppose I unhooked the chain and Booford ran down the road, I thought with a shiver. He could get killed.

I kissed Booford's head and pulled away from him. I walked sadly home, and Booford started barking again. Each bark seemed to say, "Walk! Walk!" Just as I opened the front door, I heard Mr. Wood yell, "Hey you dumb dog, shut up!"

6. Dad's Plan

"**I** think Booford cries sometimes," I said the next day at breakfast.

"Really," Dad answered, but he kept reading the paper.

"Really," I repeated.

He still did not look up. He turned the page and read some more.

"Daddy," I said, "there's a pink elephant behind your chair."

"No, there isn't," he answered, "but there's a green one behind yours." He put the paper down and swallowed a sip of coffee. "Did I hear you say that Booford cries sometimes?"

"Yes," I answered. "At least, he gets tears in his eyes."

"Well," said Dad, "I've been thinking."

"Thinking?"

"Yes," he said. "Some way I want to make

that sad, old dog happy, and thus make my daughter happy, and," he paused and cleared his throat, "and keep her home at night."

"Oh . . . you know . . . I didn't think any-one heard me." I was embarrassed so I kept talking. "I was going to let Booford run and play, but a car came by and I thought—"

"Hayley," Dad interrupted, and I knew from the tone of his voice that this was a serious conversation. "I'm not happy about what you did last night. We don't know Mr. Wood very well. It was late, after midnight, when you left this house. Besides, there are bad people, even in the country."

I felt a lump in my throat. Mom fussed at me and sometimes even yelled at me, but Dad never did. I liked him to be proud of me. "I just wanted to help Booford," I explained in a voice that had a little squeak in it. I hoped the tears that I could feel in my eyes didn't show.

Dad smiled. "It's okay," he said. He leaned across the table and smacked my head with the newspaper. I realized he had seen the tears. "As I said, I've been thinking."

"You'll think of a plan."

"I'll try." He glanced at the clock. "I've got to go," he said. "Be good."

That was a very long day. I spent most of the

time watching the clock or swinging on the porch swing and watching for Dad.

When he finally pulled into the driveway that afternoon, I ran to the car to meet him. He was carrying a leash. "Did you think of a plan?" I asked.

He nodded and handed me the leash.

"Tell me!" I shouted.

"I've thought all day," Dad began, "and I've decided the best plan is a simple one. One you probably won't appreciate. One you probably won't even call a plan."

"Well, what is it?"

"I think that if you just go over to Mr. Wood's house, knock on his door, and ask to walk the dog, he'll agree."

"I can't do that," I said. Suddenly, I felt very weak and puny . . . just from thinking about standing in front of Mr. Wood. I couldn't believe that this was Dad's plan.

"And why not?" Dad asked, and his question was serious.

"I'm a ten-year-old girl," I said. Why didn't Dad understand? "I'm just a kid."

"You can talk, can't you?" Dad answered and he smiled at me.

"Of course I can talk, but who would listen to a ten-year-old girl? And besides, Mr. Wood is big and he might get mad and yell."

"He might," said Dad. "But he might say, 'Certainly, young lady, take my dog for a walk. How kind of you to offer.' "

Sometimes my dad was dumb, very dumb. I didn't want to do what he wanted me to do, so I stood there not doing anything.

"Do you want me to go with you to talk to Mr. Wood?" he asked after a while.

I stood there trying very hard to think of some other plan, but I couldn't think of a single one.

"No," I said. "No, I'll go by myself, but you stay outside in the yard. If he kills me, come over and get my body."

Dad laughed. I smiled at him, but it was not a smile from inside. It was only on my face.

Slowly, very, very slowly, I wandered toward Mr. Wood's house.

Mr. Wood was in the driveway waxing his truck. I stood behind him for a few seconds, then quietly spoke his name. "Mr. Wood," I said. He didn't hear me.

I turned my head and looked at Dad, who lifted his right arm in a sort of wave. I moved to the side of the truck to face Mr. Wood. "Mr. Wood," I repeated a little louder. He glanced up but kept rubbing the hood. "Iamsadandlonely because Idon'thaveadog. Could I walk-Booford and pretendhewasmine."

"Slow down, kid," Mr. Wood muttered. He didn't look at me. He just kept rubbing the hood of his truck. "I don't know one word you said."

I wasn't sure I would have the nerve to say those words again. I was surprised to hear myself begin speaking. "I don't have a dog," I said, "and I am lonely and sad and I need a dog. My mom won't let me have one." I stopped to breathe. "Could I walk Booford and pretend he was mine? Walking him would make me a happy child." I looked away toward Booford.

Mr. Wood stopped waxing and wiped perspiration from his forehead with his shirt sleeve. "Kid," he said, "you don't look sad. You don't look lonely, either." He stared at me, and I stared back for a while, and then I looked down at my tennis shoes and wondered how fast they could run.

Suddenly, Booford barked his bark that sounded like "Walk! Walk!" and I felt very brave. I stood as tall as I could and I looked straight at Mr. Wood. "Mr. Wood," I said in a strong voice.

"No more lies, kid," he warned. "You aren't a very good liar."

"Mr. Wood," I said again just as forcefully as before, "Booford walks in circles and barks all night because he is bored. He is tired of being chained all the time. He wants to go for walks.

If you are too busy or too whatever to take him, then I'll walk him. He wants to run and play. It is just so dumb not to walk him. You have lived here six whole weeks and Boo hasn't had a walk. Not even one. Not even a pat on the head. Not even a 'Good Boy!' "

Mr. Wood folded his arms across his chest. His face showed no emotion for a moment, and then he started laughing. "What do you know," Mr. Wood roared. "Some skinny girl telling me I'm neglecting my dog. Some puny kid wearing pigtails telling me off. How old are you, anyway? Eight?" He laughed even louder.

My face suddenly felt fiery red. I dropped the leash. I took two steps backward and turned and raced past Booford and past my dad and into the house and past the television and up the steps and into my room. I slammed the door shut behind me and leaned against it and felt big, hot tears roll down my cheeks.

After I stopped crying, I lay on my bed looking at the flowers on the wallpaper. They were yellow and green. I don't think I had ever really looked at those flowers before.

I sniffed, sat up on the bed, blew my nose, and then lay back again. Why couldn't I just get mad and not cry? When I cried, I felt like a sissy.

For a little while longer, I lay there quietly just looking at the flowers and wondering what to do. I didn't want to go downstairs because I would see Dad. My dad was brave. He wouldn't have run away from Mr. Wood. I didn't want to go outside bcause I would see Booford and that would make me sad. I decided I would have to stay in my room for a year or two. I lay there wishing school started the next day.

Suddenly, something moved on the foot of my bed. Without moving, I looked toward my feet. There stood Herkimer. Herkie had lived in my room for several weeks now, but this was the very first time that she had come toward me instead of running away from me. I lay perfectly still.

She bumped her head against my foot and carefully moved on her three legs toward my head, sniffing my legs and clothes as she moved. When she reached my hand, I wiggled my fingers. She jumped away, but then slowly returned to my side. "Hi, Herkimer," I said softly.

I was glad to be making friends with her and yet I was sad, too. I had kind of hoped she'd stay wild; if she were wild, I wouldn't be able to catch her, so I wouldn't have to take her back to the barn. We could try to live-trap her again, but Mr. Miller had told Edward and me that trapping most animals the second time was very, very difficult. Herkimer sniffed and sniffed my fingers and then moved up my arm toward my face.

"Hayley," Dad called from downstairs. Herkie instantly bounded off the bed and disappeared. "Hayley!"

"What?" I yelled back.

"You have company . . . Mr. Wood and some sad, old dog are down here."

"Booford," I whispered aloud. I sat up on the bed. Could Mr. Wood be letting me walk Booford after all? Or maybe he had just come over to yell at me or laugh some more. But why would he bring the dog for that?

"Hayley," Dad shouted again.

I rubbed my face with my hands, hoping to wipe away tearstains, and tiptoed down the stairs. Mr. Wood was standing in the open front doorway, holding one end of my leash. Booford was on the other end of it. Mr. Wood and Daddy were talking. As I peeped around the corner, Mr. Wood saw me.

"Hey, kid," he said. "You sure left in a hurry."

I just stood there, feeling my heart beat, my mouth dry.

"Well," Mr. Wood said, "are you going to walk this dog or not?"

"Sure," I answered in an unsure, squeaky voice. I took the leash and Booford went crazy. He ran around my legs and tangled me in the leash so that when I tried to take a step I fell on the rug. He licked my face, and Dad and I laughed.

"Are you sure," Mr. Wood spoke solemnly, "are you positive you want to do this?"

"I'm sure," I said, struggling to my feet. "Dad, where should we go?"

Boo bounced back and forth, barking and jerking me left and right.

"Around the yard about twenty times," Dad suggested. "He's obviously not been to obedience school."

Booford dragged me through the front door and down the steps. I ran after him, hanging on to the leash.

Dad and Mr. Wood stood at the top of the porch stairs as Boo and I tore across the front yard, up the driveway, around the carport and the garden, and back to the front yard. At first, Boo panted and pulled, but after three trips around the yard, I was beside him, and after five trips, I was in front. We meandered around the front yard, Boo with his nose to the ground sniffing flowers and rocks and trees and grass.

"Take him to the store," Dad called as we passed. "Stay in the grass, not on the road."

The store was about a quarter of a mile west on the back road, in the opposite direction from Mr. Miller's farm. I knew Dad suggested going there because there were no hills, so he could watch us all the way there and back.

At the edge of the yard, I turned left. Boo was following, but when he faced the open road, he bounded away. I stumbled and almost fell, and then I regained my balance, shortened the leash, and hauled Boo in. He smelled honeysuckle along the fencerow, snapped at a bumblebee, and tried to veer into neighbors' yards. Sable, the Whites' old black Lab, barked and ran back and forth inside his fence. Boo trotted by, his head high. It seemed to me that he was shouting, "I am being walked! I am being walked!"

We charged all the way to the little store before Booford slowed down. On the way home, he lowered his nose to the ground and sniffed, but he always kept moving. At times he broke into a run, and I could barely keep up with his swinging tail.

When we got back to Mr. Wood's house, the sun had colored the western sky a bright red. I chained Booford to his tree. "We'll walk

again," I promised. Boo stood on his back legs and put his front legs around my waist. He licked my nose and face. I scratched around his ears. "Don't worry," I said once more, "we'll walk again."

Mr. Wood wasn't on the porch with Dad. I guessed he had gone inside his house. I decided to get the asking over with. I barged up Mr. Wood's front steps, breathed deeply, and raised my hand to knock on the door, but Mr. Wood opened it before I could.

"Could I walk him tomorrow, too?" I asked immediately. My insides were trembling.

"Sure, kid," he said. "Walk him every day." He closed the door.

7. Mr. Wood and Ruby

I raced across the road and bounded up the front porch steps. "Dad," I yelled. "Dad, he said I could walk Booford every day. Every day!" I dropped down on my knees beside Dad, who was sitting on the swing reading papers from his briefcase.

"Every day," I said again. "He told me I could walk him every day."

Dad put the papers in the briefcase and closed it. "That's great, Hayley. Great for all of us."

"Great for Booford most of all," I said. "No more being bored all the time."

"Great for Hayley," Daddy said. "No more being sad about that poor, sad old dog."

"Great for Dad," I said. "No more being worried about Hayley."

"Great for Mr. Wood," Dad said.

"What? What! Great for Mr. Wood?" Sometimes my dad was strange. Why was he thinking of Mr. Wood? Why should I do something great for mean Mr. Wood?

"Sure," Dad said. "Think about it." He moved his briefcase, and I sat down beside him on the swing. "Well?" Dad asked.

"For Mr. Wood," I said, "no new holes in his yard and less barking."

"I was thinking more along the lines of for Mr. Wood, no more being lonely."

"Hey, that's right," I said. "Now maybe he'll be friends with Booford. Maybe he'll even take Booford for walks himself."

"I wasn't thinking of Booford," Dad said. "I was thinking of a certain girl with braids. I don't think Mr. Wood has many other friends."

"I'm not surprised," I said. "Who wants a monster for a friend?"

"Hayley," Dad said seriously, "Mr. Wood is not a monster. He isn't even mean. A little unfriendly, yes. A little impolite, yes. But, Hayley, usually there are reasons for people's behavior."

"There are no good reasons for not walking your dog."

Dad smiled. "Maybe Mr. Wood has never thought about walking Booford. It might be that simple. Or it might be more complex. You know that your Aunt June won't touch dogs."

"I know."

"Did you know that when she was six, her dog Brownie got hit and killed by a car? After that, she wouldn't go near dogs. Most people think she hates dogs or she's afraid of them. Really, I think she loves them, and I guess inside she is afraid, but not of being bitten. I think she's afraid of loving another dog, because she's afraid of losing another dog."

"That's very sad," I said. "But what does all that have to do with Mr. Wood?"

"I'm just saying Mr. Wood may have a reason for being kind of unfriendly."

"I could ask him why he's mean," I said.

"Do you want Mr. Wood for a friend?" Dad questioned.

"I guess so . . . I know it seems awful bad to say so, but I want to be Mr. Wood's friend just so he'll let me be friends with Booford."

"Then don't ask him. Someday he may tell you, but don't ask him. Okay?"

"Okay."

"Besides, maybe Mr. Wood is just Mr. Wood. People do have different personalities, you know."

Dad got up and went into the house. I followed him into the kitchen. "We haven't had supper, and your mom's gone to aerobics," he said. "I don't want to cook, and I don't want a microwave dinner."

"I'll cook," I said, "if you load the dishwasher and clean up the mess."

"What can you cook?"

"Tomato sandwiches and chocolate milk," I said.

"Let's go out," Dad suggested. "I feel like a steak."

"I feel like French fries and a hot fudge sundae."

After I fed all the cats, we went into town for supper. I brought Booford Dad's steak bone.

*

That night I thought about what Dad had told me about people having reasons for acting as they do. I thought about Mr. Wood yelling at Boo and not being very friendly. I fell asleep thinking of Mr. Wood in his armchair with a heart on one arm and *Love Ruby* on the other.

I dreamed that Ruby was Mr. Wood's wife and that Booford had been her dog. Anyway, Ruby got killed and Mr. Wood grew afraid to love anybody because he was afraid they'd get killed, too. And Mr. Wood didn't like being around Boo because Boo reminded him of Ruby.

The next morning I told Daddy about the dream. "Where did you get the name Ruby?" he asked.

"It's written in purple letters on Mr. Wood's arm."

"That's a tattoo," Dad told me.

All day I wondered about Ruby. Maybe Ruby had been a girl that Mr. Wood loved. A beautiful lady with long, blonde hair. Maybe she had married Mr. Wood's best friend.

Or maybe Ruby was his sister, and when she was ten, she got lost in the woods while the family was camping and was never found again.

Dad said I should just forget about Ruby. So did Mom.

For the next two weeks, Booford and Edward and I covered miles and miles and miles. Sometimes we walked; mostly we jogged. We walked every day in the morning and sometimes in the evening. Booford still dug a few holes and still walked in a few circles—but not nearly as often. The best thing, though, was the look in his eyes. Now his eyes were shiny. Now they were happy.

One Saturday, about the middle of July, Mr. Wood was painting his porch when I got there to walk Booford. "Hi," I said. He nodded his head. I hooked the leash on Booford and started down the driveway. Boo looked back at Mr. Wood and barked and then he tried to drag me toward him. "Booford wants you to come along, I guess," I said.

Was I surprised. Mr. Wood put down his paintbrush and followed us.

We walked along quietly. At least, Mr. Wood and I were quiet. The birds seemed extra noisy, and Boo kept stopping to sniff the ground. After a while, I thought I ought to say something. I did want to be a friend to Mr. Wood. I peered at him from the corners of my eyes. *Love Ruby* bulged out on his arm as he swung it in time with his footsteps.

"Who is Ruby?" I suddenly asked.

"What?"

"You have *Ruby* written on your arm. Who is Ruby?"

"Oh, the tattoo." He slapped his arm. "Ruby was a racehorse. She used to run at Aqueduct, a racetrack in New York. I bet a hundred dollars on her, and she won me over five thousand. She had a shiny red coat and long, pretty legs. She sure was a beauty and a beautiful runner."

I giggled. "I thought she was a girlfriend."

"Well, she was my friend, I guess."

"You like horses?" I asked.

"Horses that win me money. I'm not much of an animal lover."

"Why do you own Booford, then?" I asked.

Mr. Wood didn't answer. He started to whistle a song, and I could tell that I had embarrassed him or upset him. "See that doghouse over there?" I said and I pointed toward the south. "Sable, an old black Lab, lives there."

"He was my wife's dog." Mr. Wood spoke softly.

"Just about every day that old Lab . . ." I stopped talking and walking. "Your wife? You had a wife?"

He didn't answer. We walked on. I glanced at him quickly.

"Me and my mouth," I said. "You don't have to tell me anything. I just ask too many questions. I just talk too much. My dad says I'm too curious."

"Ever hear of nosy?" Mr. Wood asked.

"Yeah." I didn't say anything else until we reached the store. Then I told him, "Most days, if we walk this way, we turn around here. I'm not supposed to go any closer to the highway than this."

"Wait here," Mr. Wood ordered, and he went inside the store. He came back with two chocolate ice cream cones. I wanted to give Boo mine, but since it had been bought for me, I thought I should eat it. I did give Boo the last part of my cone.

On the walk back I didn't talk. I was afraid Mr. Wood wouldn't walk with us again, and I wanted him to. I didn't want him to come along on every walk—I wanted some just for Boo and me—but I wanted him to come sometimes. Dad was right; he didn't seem to have many friends. Maybe none. I had never seen anyone visit his house. And since his wife was dead, maybe he needed some friends. I kept wishing I could do the walk over and not ask any questions; or at least, not ask about Mrs. Wood.

"Let's let him run," Mr. Wood said when we reached his yard. He unhooked Booford's leash and set him free before I even had time to think about what he was doing. Booford flew around the house.

"He might run away," I shouted as I started to chase after him.

"Wait," Mr. Wood commanded. Booford completed his circle of the house and when he headed toward the road, Mr. Wood whistled and called, "Here, Booford. Here boy." Booford came running up to us, his tail wagging.

"Booford isn't at all mean," I said when Mr. Wood was chaining him to the tree. "So why do you have that 'Beware of Dog' sign?"

"To keep away people," Mr. Wood replied, "especially vacuum cleaner salesmen and kids who ask too many questions." He looked down at me and laughed.

I laughed too. It was great to hear Mr. Wood laugh. "I'll send over Mr. Hillyard tomorrow," I said seriously.

"Mr. Hillyard? Who's Mr. Hillyard?"

"He sell vacuums," I told him, and when he laughed again, I did too.

Later that night I told Dad about Ruby and Mrs. Wood. Mom had gone to choir practice, and Dad and I were watching *The Black Stallion*.

"My dream was close," I said. "He's married, or he was. Anyway, Booford was her dog."

"Mr. Wood was married?"

"Yes. There was a wife, a Mrs. Wood. But he didn't say how she died."

"Did you ask?" Dad sounded serious, and he looked concerned.

"No."

"Good."

"Don't worry. I won't ask," I said. I turned sideways in my chair and let my legs dangle over the side. Smokey bumped his head against my feet. "Maybe Mr. Wood was driving a car and had a wreck and she was killed and now he can't forgive himself. Or maybe she got cancer and he sat by her bed for two years and watched her slowly die." I leaned down and scratched Smokey's head. "Or maybe—"

"Hayley," Dad interrupted.

"What?"

"You 'maybe' all you want. But don't ask. Listen if Mr. Wood tells you, but don't ask."

"Dad . . . I'm not dumb. I won't ask. Oh," I tried to sound very serious, "there is something I did ask."

RUBY

"I don't know if I want to hear this."

"Remember Ruby?"

"The tattoo?"

"Yes. She was from New York. She had beautiful red hair and long, pretty legs."

Dad's eyebrows went up. "Mr. Wood told you that?"

"Yes." I was trying not to smile.

"Did she marry Mr. Wood's best friend?"

I burst out laughing. "I hope not," I said. "Ruby was a racehorse!"

Dad chuckled, but he didn't seem to think the Ruby thing was nearly as funny as I did.

---

8. Recluse

Dad didn't have to worry about my asking Mr. Wood anything. For the next two weeks after that Saturday walk, I hardly saw Mr. Wood. It seemed as though he didn't want to talk to me anymore. Maybe he was embarrassed about telling me what he had told me. Maybe he was just tired. Maybe he just didn't want to see or talk to anybody.

All he did every day for those two weeks was drive to work, drive home, walk into the house, and tell Boo to shut up. He didn't mow his grass or wax his truck or finish painting the porch. He left the ladder and paint bucket in his front yard.

While I was walking Boo in the mornings, he left for work. When I walked Boo in the evenings, he was home, but the house was quiet.

No television or radio was on. I decided to invite him to walk with Booford and me, but when I knocked on his door, there was no answer. I knew Mr. Wood was home because I had watched him turn his truck into his driveway, get out, walk past Booford, and go into the house. His house had a front door and a side door, and I could see both from the living room window. He hadn't come out of either door, so I knew he had to be in his house, ignoring my knocking. I had even written Mr. Wood this letter:

Dear Mr. Wood,
Booford wants you to walk with us. Can you come? Also, can you swim? Edward needs some help with swimming and I need some help with diving. Please call soon. My number is 555-8325.
Sincerely,
Hayley and Edward

I had signed both our names and stuck the note between the screen door and the wooden door. I never got an answer.

Edward came over on Wednesday. He had just gotten home from computer camp. I took him with me to walk Booford. He told me about some new computer program that made charts.

I told him about Mr. Wood's wife being dead and about how Mr. Wood had been acting. I told him about the note, too.

"He doesn't want to see me anymore," I said as we crossed the first hill past my house on the way to the farm. "I don't see him except when he goes into his house after work. That's the way it's been for two weeks. This is just so weird. Before, he was talking to me, and once he came along for a walk. I even heard him laugh a little. But now he won't even come out of the house."

"Have you knocked on his door?"

"Yes, but he didn't answer, and I know he was home."

"Are you sure?"

I nodded. "I'm sure. I saw him. Once I looked in through the living room window, and there he sat holding a picture. Another time, when I didn't see him in the living room, I looked in the bedroom window, and there he was—in bed at eight o'clock in the evening. It wasn't even dark."

Edward stopped walking and stood in the middle of the road staring at me. I stopped, too, and turned to face him. "You know what," he said, "you're crazy. You could get in trouble for peeping into people's windows. Probably you could get arrested."

"Don't worry about it," I said. "Nobody saw me." Booford darted away, pulling me after him. "Dad says," I shouted back to Edward, who was running to catch up, "Mr. Wood might be depressed. He says we should get him out. Get him to do things. Dad asked him to go play golf, but Mr. Wood said he doesn't play."

I pulled Booford to a stop. "My mom says Mr. Wood should talk to a psychiatrist. Mom said he might be like Boo Radley."

"Who's Boo Radley?" Edward asked.

"She said he was this guy in a book who didn't want to have anything to do with people. She said he was a recluse. A loner. Kind of like a hermit, I think. Strange, isn't it?" I said.

"What's strange?"

"A recluse named Boo Radley," I said, "and a man who acts like Boo Radley with a Boo dog." Boo stopped suddenly to sniff through the overgrown brush on the bank beside the road. "Hey, Boo boy, what do you smell?" I asked.

"Are you going to the beach?" Edward asked me.

"In August . . . like always."

"I'll take care of your cats and walk this dog."

"I was hoping Mr. Wood would be walking him by then."

"Maybe he will," Edward said, but he didn't sound very hopeful.

"Come on, Boo. Let's go." I pulled Boo away from the honeysuckle, and we continued down the road. After we crossed the big bridge, Edward left me to check for arrowheads near the stone fence again while I let Booford go swimming in a quiet pool next to the creek. Then we walked on to Mr. Miller's farm.

We didn't see Mr. Miller. His pickup truck was gone, so we stayed for just a little while to watch his horses graze before we headed home.

"What'll we do about Mr. Wood?" I asked Edward when we got back to my house.

"I think your dad's got the right idea. I think we ought to get him out doing things. Anything. Do you think he'd like to go swimming with us? He could help me in the deep water, just like your dad."

"He never answered my letter, but I guess we could try to ask him," I said. "He can only say no, if he comes to the door." We knocked on Mr. Wood's door to ask. No one came. Edward knocked very hard and I yelled, "Mr. Wood. Hey, Mr. Wood." Still, no answer.

Edward went home and so did I. Dad had gone to a baseball game. Mom was eating popcorn and reading a book. I sat in the rocking chair worrying about Mr. Wood and wishing my mom or some adult would make sure he was okay. "He won't come out," I said after a long silence.

"What?" Mom asked, looking up from the novel she was reading.

"Mr. Wood doesn't come to the door when Edward and me knock," I explained.

"Edward and I," Mom corrected. "Hayley, are you and Edward bothering that man?"

"No, we're not bothering him. We just wanted to ask him to go swimming with us. I know he's home, and we knocked and yelled but he didn't come to the door."

Mom got another handful of popcorn and went back to reading.

"Maybe he fell in his shower," I said. "Maybe he had a heart attack."

"Didn't you tell me that the same thing happened yesterday? You knocked and he wouldn't come?"

"Yes."

"And didn't you see him this morning and he was okay?"

"Yes."

"Well, don't you think he's okay? He just doesn't want company."

"Maybe he is okay, but maybe he isn't. Maybe this time something really is wrong. Mom, would you go over there with me? If he heard a different voice, he might come to the door."

Mom almost laughed. "Hayley, I'm not going to do that," she said.

"Well, could you call the rescue squad? They could check on him."

"I'm not calling the rescue squad, either. Your dad will be here in half an hour. He can go over."

I sat on the porch steps waiting for Dad and wondering about Mr. Wood. Maybe Mr. Wood really was sick. Maybe he had caught whatever it was that had killed his wife. Maybe he was dead. I shivered. Or maybe he was just in the shower and didn't hear us when we knocked and yelled.

Boo suddenly bounced up and down and barked crazily. "Shut up, dog!" came from inside the quiet house. Well, I thought, at least I know he's not dead.

Then I saw why Booford was barking. Down the road came Edward, pulling a lawn mower behind him. I smiled. Edward was a great friend.

Edward mowed Mr. Wood's yard and I trimmed. It was almost dark when we finished and there in Mr. Wood's yard, near the road, sat two Cokes and two candy bars.

The next evening Mr. Wood waxed his truck.

I watched him from my house. His arms moved slowly as if he were tired. I wondered how he could be tired when he hadn't been doing anything.

When I got back from walking Booford, Mr. Wood was still in the yard, very slowly rubbing the hood of his truck. I said hi and he said "Hi, kid." Finally.

I didn't know why he had stopped talking to me or why he started talking again, but I didn't guess it mattered.

On Friday, Mom sent me to invite Mr. Wood to a cookout we were having that evening. His front door was open, so I figured he would answer when I knocked. I peered through the screen door. There he sat in his chair staring straight ahead. No TV on. No lights on. No newspaper. Just Mr. Wood looking at nothing and holding a picture in his hands. I watched him for maybe five minutes. Finally, he leaned back in the chair and closed his eyes, still clutching the picture.

"Mr. Wood," I called. "Hello, anybody home?"

Startled by my voice, Mr. Wood almost dropped the picture. "Come in, kid," he said.

I stepped inside the door. I felt a little shaky. Mr. Wood made me nervous. He looked

mean, probably because he needed to shave. I thought, too, that he looked sad. I didn't know what to say to a sad and mean person.

"Come here," he demanded. "I want to show you this."

I moved near his chair. I could smell his cigar.

He showed me a picture of a pretty lady with long dark hair and blue eyes. "This is Mrs. Wood."

"She's very pretty," I said.

" 'She's very pretty.' Is that all? No questions?"

"No," I said. "No questions."

Mr. Wood gazed at the picture and a smile started to come but stopped before it really was a smile.

Maybe he wants to talk, I thought. Maybe he *wants* questions. "I'm sure," I said suddenly, "I'm *sure* she's in heaven."

Mr. Wood sort of laughed.

"Don't you believe in heaven?" I asked him.

"Yeah, I believe in heaven. But she's not there . . . she's in Richmond."

"Oh, she's not . . . dead."

"No, she's not dead. She's alive and well, I guess. I haven't talked to her in six months."

I looked at the picture. There were so many questions I wanted to ask.

———

"I came home from work one day two years ago, and she was gone. There was a note—she had to find herself, it said." Mr. Wood laughed the way he had when I said Mrs. Wood was in heaven. "That wasn't an original thing to say. Everybody said that back in the sixties, when we were teenagers . . . She calls sometimes. She says, 'What are you doing?' I always say, 'Talking to you.' " Mr. Wood's voice had grown very quiet.

He placed the picture on the table and kept gazing at it. "She left Booford." He leaned back in the chair and breathed deeply.

I didn't know if he was sad or mad or what he was. I sat on the floor beside his chair. "Lots of my friends' parents are divorced," I said. "I think they do okay . . . after a while, I mean."

"We're not divorced." Mr. Wood spoke sharply. "I don't want—" He didn't finish the sentence, but I knew that what he didn't want was a divorce.

"Oh, I almost forgot," I blurted, glad to change the subject. "I came over here to invite you to a picnic tonight. Mom said just bring yourself. We'll have hamburgers, corn on the cob, potato salad, and homemade ice cream."

"Thanks for asking, but I'm busy tonight."

"Grandma's bringing her chocolate pie."

"You can take Booford, if you want to, but like I said, I'm busy." He leaned forward and turned on the television, and I got up to leave.

When I was halfway down the walk, Mr. Wood opened the door and yelled, "Hey, kid!"

I walked back up the sidewalk toward Mr. Wood and squinted in the evening sun so that I could see him clearly. "Change your mind about the picnic?" I asked.

"No. No. Forget that stuff I told you just now . . . about Jessica. I shouldn't have told you. I never told anybody before. I don't know why I told a kid."

"I won't tell anybody else," I said. "If you want me to, I could help you think of some plans . . . some ways to . . . well, get her back . . . you know."

"No, kid. Nothing doing."

"You could buy tickets for a cruise for two somewhere or rent a log cabin in the mountains and get snowed in or at least—"

"Kid, I said no."

"At least, you could send her flowers. Roses."

"Hey, I said drop it, kid," Mr. Wood almost shouted, and he closed the door. He closed the screen door and the other door both, even though it was hot outside.

———

Oh, no, I thought.

I stopped to talk to Boo. "I probably won't see him for a month now. What are we going to do, Boo? What are we going to do? We have to help him. You know that." I cradled Boo's head between my hands and scratched around his ears. Boo looked at me and wagged his tail. I think Boo understood, but he didn't know what to do either.

9. Herkimer, Again

Mom woke me at eight o'clock Saturday morning to say that Dad had gone to the hardware store and that Mr. Miller was coming to pick up Herkimer.

"Oh," I said. I was surprised. "When?"

"This morning. He just called. He said it's been six weeks." Mom put the bedroom window down and closed the curtains. "It's already hot," she said, and she turned on the air conditioner and went back downstairs.

I felt sad about Herkie's leaving. I hadn't expected Mr. Miller ever to come for her. I hadn't said anything to Mom or Dad, but I figured he would just never pick her up. Before very long, I would leave my bedroom door open, and she would live in the house with Smokey or on the porch with Dixie, and then after a long time, she'd learn to know the other cats and go outside to play. But Mr. Miller was really coming, and he was coming very soon.

I tried to be glad. Herkie had a home to go to, and, at least, I'd know where she would be, and I could visit her. The barn was warm and dry, and the fields made good places to play, places far away from cars. And Mr. Miller fed his cats twice a day.

But then I remembered that Mr. Miller's cats didn't get any vaccinations. His barn cats probably had fleas and ear mites and worms. And his barn cats were not spayed or neutered. They always had lots and lots of kittens.

I lay there a little longer thinking a little more until one of my good thoughts almost turned into a bad one—Herkie had come to me from the farm with a broken leg, a shattered-into-tiny-pieces leg, and I had called the farm a good place to play.

I got up and searched my dresser for some shorts and a top. Still, I thought, most of the time living at the farm probably was safer than living at my house, just because my house was a lot closer to the road. Also, people drove faster by my house than by Mr. Miller's farm because the road in front of my house was hard-surfaced, and the road by the farm was dirt. I felt better.

I got dressed, ran down the stairs, fed Smokey and Dixie, and went outside to feed the other cats. Everybody came except Roby. Sometimes she missed breakfast so I wasn't worried.

After the cats were fed, I sat on Dad's lawn chair to wait for Mr. Miller and tried to think of some reason why Herkimer shouldn't leave. I thought I had settled the Herkimer thing with myself before I left my bedroom, but I still wanted to keep her.

The fact that Herkie had only three legs wasn't a very good reason for her to stay. She did fine on three legs in my bedroom, so I guessed she'd do fine on three legs in Mr. Miller's barn. I couldn't think of any good reason why she shouldn't leave except that I wanted her to be spayed and get her vaccinations, and I didn't think Mr. Miller would do these things.

Mom came outside with a glass of chocolate milk. She sat down beside my feet on the end of the lawn chair and handed me the glass. "Here," she said, "you didn't eat." She paused and then added, "You want to keep her, don't you?"

I nodded.

"Mr. Miller takes good care of his animals," Mom said. "She'll be okay. In fact, that farm is a better place for her than this house. You know Hairy—he'd probably fight with her."

"I hadn't thought of that. But she could stay

inside with Smokey or on the porch with Dixie." I took a big gulp of milk. "Mom," I continued, "Mr. Miller doesn't get his cats any shots and he doesn't get them spayed. I don't think he has extra money to spend on the cats."

"I think he has enough money," Mom answered. "He probably just doesn't believe in getting cats spayed. People didn't use to do that, you know."

Our discussion was stopped right there. Dad drove into our driveway, and Mr. Miller was behind him. Mr. Miller got out of his pickup truck and lifted a cat carrier from the bed of the truck.

"Good morning everybody," he said, handing me the carrier. "Can you catch her?"

"Usually I can," I said.

Mom, Dad, and Mr. Miller stayed in the yard talking. I went up to my room alone. Herkie was asleep on my bed. I stroked her soft fur and picked her up and held her close and rocked her back and forth. "Be good, Herkimer," I said. "I'll visit you real often. I'll come every Saturday in the summer and whenever I can during the winter." I kissed her on the top of her head. "I'll ask Mr. Miller if I can get you spayed. And get your shots."

I was hoping she would struggle and escape

and hide under my bed, but putting her into the cat carrier was easy; she didn't fight at all. Then she started meowing very loudly.

"It's okay, Herkimer," I whispered. "It's okay."

There was a soft tap on my bedroom door. "Catch her?" Dad asked quietly from the other side.

"Yes," I said as I opened the door.

Dad stood there smiling. "She'll be fine," he said. "But will you?"

"Yes," I said and I breathed deeply. "I wouldn't mind this much at all if I knew she would be spayed and get her shots." I put the carrier on the floor and sat down on the bed. "Could I tell Mr. Miller that we'd pay for that to be done?"

"I don't know," Dad said as he shook his head no. "Mr. Miller has money, Hayley . . . more than we do by a long ways. And it's not that I mind paying for a cat to be spayed, but Mr. Miller might feel insulted if we offered."

"Suppose I paid for her shots and the operation," I said. "I could wash people's cars or weed gardens, or"—I made a face—"I could help people clean their houses."

"You would clean houses?"

I nodded. "Yeah." I hated even thinking about mopping kitchens and dusting furniture, but I would do it.

Dad laughed. "I guess," he said, "it would be all right for you to ask."

I carried the carrier downstairs and outside and set it in the grass near Mr. Miller. He tried to hand me a ten-dollar bill. "No," I said. "Don't pay me. It was fun taking care of her."

"Take it," he said. "I owe you more than that just for food."

I looked at Dad and at Mr. Miller. Mr. Miller had been my friend for a long time. I would take a chance. "Okay," I said. "I'll take the ten dollars if you'll drive Herkie and me to Dr. Rhodes and let me use it to get her rabies shot. Is that okay?"

"Hayley!" Mom sounded stern.

"Not necessary," said Mr. Miller. "She—"

"But all cats need rabies shots," I interrupted.

"What I wanted to say was she already had a rabies shot, and—"

"What?" I interrupted again. "What did you say?"

"I said she already had a rabies shot. Dr. Rhodes gave her that the day I picked her up from the clinic and brought her here. He said I ought to get her spayed, too. He said having

a litter of kittens would be kind of hard on a little cat with three legs. So, I guess we'll get that done, too. When she's old enough."

"That's great, Mr. Miller," I said. I could hardly believe what I had heard. All my worries had disappeared in an instant. "I'll catch her for you," I said, "when it's time. And if you want me to, I'll keep her again in my room for a while after the operation."

Mr. Miller extended his hand. "Deal," he said, "if . . . and only if . . . you accept this ten dollars and spend it on yourself." We shook hands then, and he backed out of our driveway with one loudly meowing kitten in a cat carrier on the seat beside him.

I ran to the edge of the yard. "Mr. Miller," I shouted. "Mr. Miller! Could I visit her this evening?"

"Sure," he shouted back. "Anytime. Come anytime." He headed down the back road.

Edward came over in the evening, and he and Booford and I walked to Mr. Miller's farm. Edward thought it was silly to be going to see Herkie so soon, but he went along anyway.

Edward helped me slide the barn door open. Pigeons roosting high in the rafters were startled and noisily fluttered about before resetting on their perches. Edward pushed the door shut behind me and waited outside with Booford.

The barn was quiet and dark with only a little sunlight filtering through slits near the highest rafters. I waited a while before calling Herkimer, because I was afraid she wouldn't come. Then, very softly, I called, "Herkie, Herkimer." No kitty came. I sat down on a bale of hay and called again a little louder. Then I heard her meowing from the top of a small stack of hay bales. "Hi, Herkie," I said. She didn't run when I moved close to her, and she even let me lift her from the hay and hug her. She purred, but then she struggled to be free. When I put her back on the hay, she darted across the bales, stopping now and then to bat playfully at loose stems of hay. She was fine.

Edward, Booford, and I walked home right away so that we'd be there before dark. Along the way, Edward talked about some space flight videos his mom had bought for him.

When we got to my house, the sun was almost down, so Edward walked on home. After I tied Booford, I knocked on Mr. Wood's door. I had been so busy with Herkie that I really hadn't thought about it, but I hadn't seen Mr. Wood all day. I knocked and knocked until my hand hurt, but he didn't come. The house was dark, so I guessed he had gone to bed already. It wasn't even nine o'clock.

For a long time that night, I couldn't go to sleep. I was thinking about Herkie and about Mr. Wood when I heard picky noises from under my bed. I looked over the edge of the mattress and saw a white face sticking out from under the bed, looking up at me. "Hi, Smokey," I said. After a little while, I felt something land on the foot of my bed. A furry, purring body lay down beside me. I fell asleep smiling.

10. Helping Mr. Wood

I sat in church beside my dad trying to listen to what the minister was saying, but my mind wouldn't stay on the words. The minister was talking about Joseph and his brothers, but I don't know what else he said because I was busy thinking about Roby.

Roby hadn't come to eat Sunday morning. For her not to be home on Saturday night might be okay—she might have been hunting or she might have been asleep somewhere. But for her still to be gone on Sunday morning meant something was wrong. I was going to hunt for Roby after church.

All during church, my mind did the *maybes*. Maybe Roby had been hit by a car and had dragged herself under the front porch and died. Maybe she had gotten caught in a leg trap. During the winter hunters set traps along Smith Creek and along the little stream. Maybe someone had left a trap in one of those places. Or maybe Roby had wandered into someone's garage, and they had shut her up inside and gone away for the weekend.

As soon as church was over, Mom, Dad, and I hurried home. Mom put the meat loaf in the oven and the potatoes and some green beans on to cook while I cleaned carrots and sliced cucumbers for the tossed salad. Then, while the potatoes were cooking, I began the search for Roby.

I decided to look first along the little stream, which flowed through the pasture field near Mr. Wood's house. It was the same stream that ran under the little bridge where Edward and I stood to watch frogs and turtles on the way to Mr. Miller's farm. At some point, it flowed into Smith Creek. There was a large grassy area along the stream shaded by a weeping willow and some other gigantic trees where I sometimes found my cats playing. I wanted to look there.

I climbed the fence and hurried down the slope toward the stream, trying not to think about the little green snakes I might be tramping on or over. Once I reached the stream, I followed it west toward the highway. It was only a few feet wide, but huge trees and tangles of briars and wild roses grew along its banks. As I trudged along, I kept calling over and over for Roby. The stream ran quietly except in a few spots where it gurgled over rocks. I listened very intently for a kitty's cry, and when I was near the clearing, I thought I heard a meow.

What I had heard was not a cat. Mr. Wood was there in the shady area sitting on a rock with his radio beside him. His head was bent forward, his hands covering his face. It looked as though he was crying. I saw his shoulders trembling and heard what I thought were sobs.

Very quietly, I lifted one foot and stepped back, then the other. I quickly turned and raced across the field toward home. I had to get help. Somebody had to do something. A grown man was sitting under a tree crying. That wasn't right. Where was his stupid wife anyway? Didn't she care? I was out of breath when I reached the top of the hill, and as I scrambled over the fence, I snagged my shorts and scraped the inside of my right leg.

When I burst through the kitchen door, Mom looked up from mashing the potatoes. "Find her?" she asked.

I shook my head no. I was panting and couldn't talk for a few seconds. "Quick, Mom," I whispered. "Where's Dad?"

"Upstairs. What's wrong? Is Roby hurt?"

I ran into the living room and shouted up the steps. "Dad! Hey, Dad! Come, quick. I found Mr. Wood down by the little stream, and I think . . ." Suddenly I wondered if I could be wrong. Maybe what I'd heard had been the radio. "I think," I shouted up the steps, "I'm not sure . . . but I think he was crying."

"What?" Dad asked as he came down the stairs.

"Mr. Wood is sitting down by the little stream. I found him when I was hunting for Roby. Dad, I think he was crying. I think he was sitting on a rock, crying." I collapsed onto the rocking chair.

Mom and Dad didn't say anything. They stood in the doorway just staring at me.

"Well?" I said.

No one said a word. I looked from Mom to Dad and from Dad to Mom.

"Well," I repeated, "what are we going to do?"

"Hayley," Mom said, "sometimes men cry. It's okay for a man to cry. Sometimes it's the best thing anybody can do."

"But I want to help . . . I want us to do something to help." I couldn't believe we were just going to ignore a man so sad.

"We care about Mr. Wood, Hayley, but I don't think he wants our help," Dad said.

"But we've got to do something." I clenched my fists.

"I'll call Reverend Moore tomorrow and ask him to visit Mr. Wood," Mom said.

"He doesn't need Reverend Moore," I said. "He needs Jessica."

"Hayley," Dad said, "we don't always get what we want—not even when we try our hardest."

"But, Dad, he's not trying at all."

"I think," Mom said firmly, "that you should just forget about Mr. Wood and Jessica. You don't know what happened between them and it's really not your business. Why don't you just walk Booford and let Mr. Wood be."

I felt a lump in my throat and looked down at my own hands to hide the tears I knew were in my eyes. "Maybe he's going to kill himself," I mumbled.

Dad and Mom looked at each other. Dad turned and quickly left the house. "John," Mom called after him, but Dad didn't answer. Mom looked at me and shook her head. "Hayley," she said, "honey, I really do think you're over-reacting."

I went into the kitchen and poured iced tea for Mom and me. Then I went outside and crossed the road to sit with Booford and wait for Dad.

Dad came back very soon, after maybe ten minutes, and he was smiling. "Mr. Wood is going to play first base for my team this afternoon," he said as I came back across the road. "Now, let's eat."

"I guess that's good," I said, following Dad into the house. "What exactly did you all say to each other?"

He sat down at the kitchen table and drank some iced tea before he answered.

"Mr. Wood was sitting there on the rock. He was peeling bark off branches with a pocket-knife and listening to his radio. I told him we needed another softball player this afternoon and he said he'd come." Dad paused. "Now, pass the potatoes, please, Hayley."

I passed the potatoes. "But why was he sitting down in the field on a rock?" I asked.

"Didn't you ever want to go off and be by yourself away from the whole world?" Dad asked me.

"Yes," I said.

"That's probably what Mr. Wood was doing today."

"But Dad, he's alone all the time. He's alone in that house every day after work. He doesn't have to go off somewhere to be by himself because he's always by himself all the time."

"I know," Dad said. "But maybe he wanted to be *outside* by himself. If he sits outside on his porch, some neighbor child that I happen to know usually goes over to talk to him."

I smiled. "Do you think that Jessica still loves him?" I asked.

"Hayley," Mom answered, "I told you before, that is not your business. And even if it were, if Jessica doesn't love Mr. Wood, there's nothing we can do to change that."

Dad looked up from his dinner. "I agree," he said. "We can't make Jessica love Mr. Wood. But there is something we can do. We can be Mr. Wood's friends." Dad looked from Mom toward me. "Hayley, you probably think that's not much of anything, but it really is, and honestly, if there were more we should do, I'd help you do it. . . . Now, we forgot the blessing, and you need to eat."

I said the blessing, but I didn't eat very much dinner.

Roby came home late in the afternoon just

before Mom, Dad, Mr. Wood, and I left for the ball game. Mr. Wood didn't talk to Mom, Dad, or me except to answer questions, and he didn't look at us much either. All the way to the game and all the way back, he stared out the window, looking at everything as if he had never driven through our town before. I figured he was thinking about Jessica.

Sometimes I wish I didn't care about dogs that don't get walked, cats that don't have homes, or people who are sad. Maybe Edward is right. Maybe I am ridiculous, sometimes.

All I could think about was Mr. Wood and his broken heart. In spite of what Mom said, I had to make certain Jessica knew that Mr. Wood wanted her back. Maybe she already knew, and if she knew and still didn't care—well, that was the end of that. But maybe she *didn't* know. Maybe she thought he didn't love her anymore. Maybe if she did know . . . Maybe if someone told her . . .

Getting Jessica's phone number was easy. We had learned about using Information in the third grade. I just dialed 1-804-555-1212. A man said, "What city, please?"

"Richmond," I answered matter-of-factly.

He said, "May I help you?"

In the next five minutes, I memorized Jessica's telephone number. I pushed all but the last digit at least fifteen different times and then hung up. Probably I had five minutes left before my mom got home from the store. Once again, I dialed the number. This time I touched the last digit too. The phone rang.

Don't answer, don't answer, don't answer, rang inside my head between each ring. I suddenly felt warm all over and nervous and almost sick.

"Hello." The voice was a woman's.

"Is this Jessica?" I asked. I could hear a quiver in my voice.

"Yes, it is. Who's calling, please?"

For a second I couldn't speak.

"Who is this?" she asked again, her voice sounding a little annoyed.

"A friend of Mr. Wood's. I called to tell you— I wanted you to know—I just . . ." My heart was beating so loudly that I couldn't think. I wished I had written down what I wanted to say.

"Is something wrong with Ben?" Her voice was tense.

"No. Yes. Well, he's . . . he still . . ."

"Who is this, anyway?"

I heard Mom's car pull into the driveway.

"Mr. Wood still loves you," I said in a rush.

"I've got to go. I shouldn't have called." I hung up the phone and ran upstairs to my room. My cheeks were burning fiery hot. Mom was coming up the stairs. I fell on my bed, buried my hot face in a pillow, and pretended to be asleep. Smokey came and bumped his head against my arm, but I didn't move.

That evening I walked Booford before Mr. Wood got home from work. I knew what I had to do, and I wanted to get it over with as soon I could.

From where Booford and I waited on his porch steps, I spotted his truck when he turned onto the back road from the highway. I felt as nervous as I had when I made the call. "This is silly," I said aloud to Booford. "I didn't really tell her anything that wasn't true. I don't know why I'm scared." But my hands trembled when I patted Boo's head.

Mr. Wood parked the truck and trudged toward the house. I stood up. I had to get it over with, now. I yelled each word carefully. "I called her."

"You did what?" Mr. Wood questioned as he crossed the yard.

"I told her you still loved her." I held my breath.

"Her?" For only a second Mr. Wood wore a

puzzled look. Then he shouted, "JESSICA?"

I nodded.

His eyes turned dark, and he slammed his lunch box to the ground. It fell open and iced tea poured from his thermos onto the grass. He grabbed my shoulders and his fingers dug into my skin. "I told you to drop it," he said. "That woman left on her own. If she comes back, it will be . . . it must be . . . on her own. You go home and you take that dog with you. I never want to see you or that woman's dog again!" He almost spit the words at me.

Sobbing, I sank down onto the steps, my head in my arms. "Please," I cried. "Please, don't be mad. I only wanted to help."

"Get out of here!" he demanded in a voice like thunder.

At the sound of Mr. Wood's shout, Booford jerked away from me and raced across the yard. I stood up and jumped off the steps after him. "Boo!" I screamed when I saw the car.

I ran fast. I ran very fast. I heard brakes and a screech, and I saw Boo in my yard and my dad running to meet us and I heard him yelling, "No! No!"

Then I saw myself in slow motion—as if I were in a movie—turning and falling and tumbling and sliding across the pavement. I couldn't stop myself, which wasn't surprising because I didn't really feel my body or my hands or any part of me and the road bumping together.

Then the movie stopped, and I was part of the world again. Dad was there, and Booford stood over me licking my face. Dad looked blurry and he was whispering from far away, "You're okay, Hayley. You're okay. You're okay. You're okay." Slowly Dad became clear and so did an old lady I didn't know. She must have been driving the car, I realized. She knelt beside me, crying.

"I'm all right," I said. "Really . . . don't cry." I started to get up, but Dad, who was on the other side of me, gently pushed my shoulders back down.

I suddenly remembered why I had been running and I realized then that Booford was missing. "Boo? Dad, where did Booford go? He was here, just now, licking my face."

"He's fine. He's just fine. Mr. Wood took him to tie him up."

"But, Dad, you don't understand," I sobbed. "Mr. Wood kicked me and Booford out. He doesn't want to see us anymore. Please Dad, get Booford. Let him live with us. Please, Dad."

"Shhh. It's okay. Calm down, baby. Mr.

Wood isn't mad at anybody . . . not you . . . not Booford." Dad gently squeezed my shoulders. "Now, Hayley," he said, "you have to go to the hospital—just to be checked. The rescue squad's coming. Don't be frightened, okay?"

I heard the siren. "Oh, Dad," I said. "I'm okay. I don't need to go. I don't want to go." Then I felt dizzy, as if I had done one hundred cartwheels in a row. "I just need a nap," I mumbled. But the sky turned dark and seemed to have golden fringes, and Dad's voice was far away.

After what seemed like a long time—but I think it was only a minute or two, because when the sky was light again the rescue squad's siren was still blowing—Dad was clear and Mom was with him. I lifted myself up on my elbows. I wasn't dizzy anymore, but my ankle felt like it had been kicked or run over.

"I don't need to go to the hospital," I protested. "The car didn't hit me. It just made me fall. And I'm okay." I didn't mention my ankle.

Dad smiled at me and kissed my forehead. Mom and he rode in the ambulance with me to the hospital. I felt like a baby. I would rather have had Edward along.

The emergency room doctor said that I had to stay overnight for observation. I had some torn muscles or ligaments or something in my ankle, a bump on my head, lots of bruises, and some bad scrapes on my legs and arms. I had to use crutches. I didn't need them, but the doctor said I had to use them for a week. Worst of all, I had to stay a second night in the hospital because the morning nurse said I had a fever.

Edward, Mr. Miller, Dr. Rhodes, Grandma, and Aunt Debbie came to visit me on the second night. Mr. Wood didn't come. Dad said he had followed the ambulance to the hospital and spent the first night in the hall outside my room. When morning came, he left, and no one saw him around the hospital after that. I was hoping he would come or call or send me a balloon or do something. But he didn't. I thought of calling him just to say hello. But I didn't.

11. In the Doghouse

On my first day home from the hospital, I waited on our porch steps for Mr. Wood to come outside. I couldn't do it. I tried to listen to the birds chattering in the front yard trees, and I even went back inside the living room and got a cat magazine to read. But nothing worked. After only ten minutes of waiting, I hobbled on my crutches across the road.

Booford saw me coming and started barking and jumping around. I laid my crutches on the ground, and he stood and put his paws around my waist and licked my face. "Booford, Booford," I said and I scratched around his ears and shook his paw and hugged him tightly.

Mr. Wood came out the front door holding Booford's leash. He stopped abruptly when he saw me.

"Hello," I said.

He nodded his head and hooked the leash on Booford's collar. "You coming?" he questioned without looking back at me.

"If you don't go too fast. I'm not very fast with these crutches."

From Mr. Wood's house to the bench near the little store, neither of us spoke a word. I swung along behind Mr. Wood; now and then, he glanced back at me. "Sit," he ordered when we reached the bench.

I sat down. He sat down. Booford stood nearby.

"Kid," Mr. Wood said, "I'm not a talker. Never have been. Never will be. But I've got to say a few words to you."

"I shouldn't have called," I said fast. "I'm sorry."

"Don't interrupt."

I nodded. I looked over at Mr. Wood, but he was staring straight ahead.

"First," he continued, "I am sorry about your ankle. Second, I want to keep Booford. Third, I called Jessica. We talked. Nothing's changed. Fourth, be my friend, but no more plans. Okay?"

"Okay."

We sat there again. No one said a single word. I wondered what we were doing. Boo lay quietly between Mr. Wood's feet and mine. I reached down and scratched his head.

Mr. Wood made a funny noise. "There is one more thing," he said. I turned, and this time he was looking down at his hands.

"I found out something when you and that car . . ." He paused for a long, long time, and I thought I might never find out what he had found out. "I found out," he said finally, "that I'm still alive."

"Still alive . . . That's dumb. Of course you're alive."

He turned and looked right at me. "What I mean is, when Jessica left and didn't come back, I didn't care about anything—about myself, about anybody, about anything. Sometimes I felt sorry for myself, but even if my best buddy died, I wouldn't have cared. Then when you were hurt, I thought I would go crazy." He stopped and looked at his hands, then back at me. "So . . . thank you."

I smiled, and Mr. Wood looked away from me again. "You're welcome," I said, "but I don't know if you should thank me."

"Why is that?"

"Aren't you saying I helped you care about other people?"

"Yes."

"Well, caring isn't always fun," I said. "I care about a lot of cats and some people, and sometimes I wish I didn't. It's not very fun sometimes. Sometimes, it's more trouble than anything."

Mr. Wood pulled Booford close to him and scratched the top of his head. "Sometimes," Mr. Wood said quietly, "it's worth the trouble."

On the walk home, I told Mr. Wood about catching Herkimer, and about letting her go, and about Smokey hanging upside down from my box spring. I knew he could only stand so much serious talk, especially about himself.

That night Edward and I sat on the porch steps. It was late. Almost ten o'clock.

"Your mom will be worried," I said.

"She knows where I am. Anyway, she said I could stay up and watch the *Star Trek* rerun."

The moon had just risen over the mountain and looked like a huge, orange beach ball. I rested my head on my knees and listened to the sounds of the summer night: crickets and the rustle of leaves in the breeze.

"Hey, Hayley," Edward almost shouted, "I forgot to tell you—Mr. Wood said he'd take me swimming next Saturday."

"Your mom's letting you go? She doesn't know Mr. Wood very well."

"I know. But she said yes, and then last night she said something about going along."

"Oh, no," I said, thinking about Edward's getting embarrassed.

"I already told her I can swim in deep water," Edward said. He sounded proud.

"Well, what did she say?"

"Not a word. She just looked worried. Are you still going to the beach?" Edward asked.

"Yes. I can go in the ocean if I'm careful."

"I guess I better go," Edward said. He went home then, and I was left alone on the porch. I didn't mind.

A cloud passed over the moon, covering all but a sliver of it, but I could still see Mr. Wood's house; it was dark. I wondered if Mr. Wood would keep walking Booford. I wondered if he and Jessica would get back together.

The front door opened and Dad came out and sat down on the porch swing. "Are you okay?" he asked.

I looked up at the stars. "Just wondering," I said. "I told Mr. Wood, or I tried to tell him, that I was sorry about calling Jessica. He told me he was sorry about my ankle."

"You all are friends again, then?"

"I guess, but I'm not supposed to do any-thing—to help, I mean. I'm not supposed to come up with any more plans, and I won't. I said I wouldn't and I won't. But it's pretty awful. Mr. Wood is just going to sit over there and get older and older and older and older."

"Well, Hayley, that's Mr. Wood's choice. He's doing exactly what he wants to do."

"But he's not doing anything, Dad. Not anything. Not one teeny, tiny thing."

"Yes, he is," Dad insisted. "He's doing exactly what he wants to. He's waiting."

"Waiting. Waiting! That's not doing anything. That's nothing."

"For a nothing, waiting sure is hard to do."

I sighed. Pinkie came and stood on my knees and bumped my chin with his head. I scratched around his ears. "What's Mr. Wood going to do?" I asked. "Wait forever?"

"Maybe. Maybe not. But that's his choice."

Silently, we waited, Dad and I, just listening to the night and feeling the warmth of a summer night in Virginia.

"You've been out here a long time. Are you okay?" Dad asked again.

"You asked me that once already."

"Sorry. Answer it again."

"Yes, I'm okay."

"Well, I'm going in to watch the news. Don't be too long."

When Dad was in the house, I picked up my crutches and crossed the road to see Booford. Mr. Wood's truck was in the driveway, and since his house was dark, I guessed he had already gone to bed. I hoped Booford wouldn't bark and wake him.

Booford didn't bark because he wasn't there. As I started to wonder where he could be, I heard from far away footsteps on the pavement and other sounds I couldn't identify. Dad's words, *There are bad people, even in the country,* popped into my head. Quickly I laid my crutches in the grass and crawled into Boo's doghouse.

The footsteps came closer and closer and the sounds became clear . . . dog claws clicking on the pavement and a dog's panting. Then jogging shoes were visible in the doghouse doorway, and I could hear Mr. Wood hooking Booford's chain. "Night, boy," Mr. Wood said.

I should have said something then, but it seemed really ridiculous to crawl out of someone's doghouse and say, "Good evening. I heard you coming. I thought you were robbers or kidnappers so I hid in your doghouse." I just stayed inside the doghouse and kept my mouth shut.

Boo must have smelled me. He danced back

and forth and dived into the doghouse. Then he sat across my lap and kept licking my face. The doghouse started to seem crowded, and I suddenly started to feel itchy and hot.

For a long, long time, I squirmed under the weight of Booford and petted him and tried to listen for the sound of a door being shut. I never heard it, but when I peeped out, I could see no lights. I supposed that Mr. Wood had already gone inside the house and gone to bed.

I crawled out the doghouse door and across the grass toward my crutches. Booford followed me. The Zirkles' pole light illuminated the area where the crutches lay.

"Hey, kid." The voice came from the front porch. I couldn't see Mr. Wood, but I sure could hear him. Then I heard laughter, very loud laughter.

I sat down in the grass and started laughing too. I was laughing at the ridiculous picture Mr. Wood must have seen: me crawling along in the grass with a dog following along behind. But I also was laughing just because Mr. Wood was laughing.

Then I got my crutches and headed home.

"Good night, Hayley," Mr. Wood called.

"Good night, good night," I said, once for Mr. Wood and once for Booford.

My dad was standing on the front porch waiting for me. "What's so funny?" Dad asked.

"I guess I am," I said.

When I went up to my room to go to bed, I leaned for a few minutes against the windowsill. I could see Booford lying asleep in the grass near his doghouse. I whispered toward the moon, which was partly blocked by branches of the elm tree, "Dear God, please bless Mom and Dad and Roby and Pinkie and Smokey and Dixie and Hairy and Herkimer and Edward and Mr. Wood and Boo and, God, I guess you better bless Jessica, too. Amen."

Suddenly, I was very tired and very happy at the same time. I dropped into my bed, which felt cool and soft. Smokey was there beside me purring loudly. I shut my eyes and pulled him close. "I want to purr too," I told him, and I made myself laugh out loud when I tried.

About the Author and Illustrator

SUSAN MATHIAS SMITH was born in Virginia and has lived there nearly all her life. She was raised on a farm and has always loved all kinds of animals. The recipient of a B.A. in English and an M.Ed. in School Library Media Services from James Madison University, Ms. Smith is Coordinator of Media Services and Public Affairs for the Shenandoah County Public Schools. She lives in the country, with many cats and dogs.

ANDREW GLASS has illustrated many picture books, some of which he wrote himself. He has recently done jacket and interior illustrations for two other Clarion novels, David Gifaldi's *Gregory, Maw, and the Mean One* and Al Carusone's *Don't Open the Door After the Sun Goes Down*. Mr. Glass lives in New York City.